I0718220

CAPTIVE OF THE HITMAN

HITMEN #4

ALEXIS ABBOTT

Copyright © 2022 Pathforgers Publishing and Alexis Abbott

First published in 2016 as Captive of the Hitman by Alexis Abbott

All rights reserved. No part of this publication may be reproduced, distributed, or transmitted in any form or by any means, including photocopying, recording, or other electronic or mechanical methods, without the prior written permission of the publisher, except in the case of brief quotations embodied in critical reviews and certain other noncommercial uses permitted by copyright law. For permission requests, write to the publisher, addressed "Attention: Permissions Coordinator," at the address below.

Pathforgers Publishing

legal@pathforgers.com

www.pathforgers.com

This is a work of fiction. Names, characters, business, events and incidents are the products of the author's imagination. Any resemblance to actual persons, living or dead, or actual events is purely coincidental. This book is intended for sale to Adult Audiences only.

Cover Design: Pathforgers Publishing

Get an EXCLUSIVE book, **FREE** just as a thank you for signing up for my newsletter! Plus you'll never miss a new release, cover reveal, or promotion!

http://alexisabbott.com/newsletter

PART OF ALEXIS ABBOTT'S HITMAN SERIES

READING ORDER:

Don't miss out on the rest of the Hitman Series by Alexis Abbott! Now available on all ebook retailers, in paperback format, and now becoming available in audiobook!

Owned by the Hitman
Sold to the Hitman
Saved by the Hitman
Captive of the Hitman
Stolen from the Hitman
Hostage of the Hitman
Taken by the Hitman

CHAPTER 1

MIKHAIL

My cock throbs in my hand as I stare at the page in a glossy magazine. It's not like I need it. It's not about her, the sexy woman sprawled along the centerfold. Even jerking off is all business.

My veins pulse as my grip tightens, and I lick my lips as I start to stroke myself. It's a slow, rhythmic thing, letting the tension gather in my shoulders. I need to feel tense now so that later, I can find the perfect calm I need.

Not too fast. Slow. Teasing. My thumb gathers the precum at the tip, running it along my swollen head, adding a hint of lubrication. It's been too long since I've been with a woman, by my own choice. I don't have room in my life for a girl, not even a fling. My job is too dangerous to drag someone into, even if I wanted that.

So instead, I stroke myself to a skin mag and groan as the stress keeps building in my gut. I have a big job tonight. Something important, and nothing can distract me, especially not this damn *urge* to fuck. To go to a club, find some hot piece of ass, and take her. Meaningless, useless, unfulfilling sex, but it'd be something.

I grip myself harder as I lean back on the couch, the tension travelling from my shoulders down to my back and into my belly. I force it lower, so that when I start jerking myself faster, I can rid myself of this fucking stress.

Gritting my teeth, my breathing speeds up, and I close my eyes. The centerfold doesn't do much for me. Most women don't.

So instead, I just focus on the feel of my hard cock, pulsing like mad in my hand. This is what life should be made of. Pleasure exploding in my brain as I get closer and closer to the edge.

And when finally I burst, my entire body empties. It's not just my balls as they tighten and spurt their cream over my abs. It's not just my mind that clears of its fog.

My entire *body* feels lighter for that perfect, pure moment of orgasm, and I'm ready to do my job tonight. There's no room for error. There's no fucking this up.

Tonight, I'm a killer.

THE GROUP of revelers spills out of the limousine. All but one are men, dressed in expensive tailored suits, ties mostly loosened. They look like they just came from Wall Street, pretentious and full of themselves and whatever perceived victory they'd just been celebrating.

Some of them hold bottles of ridiculously expensive booze, but it's clear that a few of them are on something much harder, looking wired. But it's the sole woman in the group that catches my attention once the others are tallied.

I hate excess casualties in my line of work. It's an increased risk, and one I don't care to take. The other men are all on my list, but this woman? A young blonde, in high heels and a red dress? She's stumbling a bit but somehow managing to make it look gracefully natural. She's had more intoxicants than she's realized, I can tell. I've seen that vaguely confused look before.

By my reckoning, one of those shit heads has slipped her something extra into her drink before they head up to the penthouse for the real party.

All targets accounted for, and one extra person isn't too much for me to handle, not even close. But there's something about her, that bright smile upon her face, the twinkle in her eyes. She doesn't strike me as the usual sort of drugged-up bimbo these sorts of guys haul back for their debauchery. There's a spark to her.

I push her from my mind though. I have to, there's no other option. Civilian casualties are sometimes an unavoidable thing. I've seen that firsthand more often than I care to remember.

It isn't long before the group has all vanished into the posh hotel, their security detail trailing behind. They do a good job looking like part of the group, for what it's worth, but there's no way for them to match the drunken, drugged-up gait while doing their job effectively, so it's easy to tell how many I have to deal with.

Six armed guards. I was expecting eight, but it seems two remain with the vehicle.

Now it's my turn.

There's no rush. My movements are casual. The last

thing I ever want to do is stand out on a mission like this, so while I have plenty of time, I don't hurry. I make my way around back, down into the subterranean parking lot.

I sight the two guards at the vehicle; one's smoking, the other's talking on a phone. They look casual too, but it's a ruse. They're alert and dangerous, like me. I stay far enough away that I never draw their eyes. My target is the door leading up.

Through the stairwell, I make my way to an employee's only hall. The key card lock is easy enough to bypass, and I just move on through. It winds through a laundry room, but nobody pays me any mind. The hotel is far too bustling for me to stand out, dressed in a black sweater and pants. I look like just another employee coming on or off the job before getting into uniform.

I swipe an access card from some manager, too busy berating an employee to notice its loss. This is something I could've done earlier in preparation, but that would have ran the risk of it being noticed. And while I doubt it'd have affected the mission, you never know with people.

But me? I know I'd have no issue getting what I need when I need it.

A service elevator takes me up, the stolen key card granting me easy access to the penthouse suites on top.

The doors open, and I walk along a narrow service hallway before peering out into the elite foyer. There, I see two more of the guards outside a door. Not that I needed to know that—it was easy to figure out which room they'd be staying at ahead of time.

I grasp a cleaning cart and roll it out into the hall to one of the rooms. It's unoccupied, and the two security men pay me little heed as I disappear inside. I suppose I look like a janitor in their eyes, harmless. Someone weak and easy to ignore, with my head and shoulders hunched, ID card dangling from my belt.

It takes me a while to meander my way on up, but still I have ample time.

I pull a knife from beneath my pant leg and slide it into my belt. I give the gun in my pocket a final check. It's small, but it'll do the job. The silencer from my other pocket screws on, and I slide my mask on down over my face. Then that's it. No time like the present.

But it's not the door I go for. That'd leave two corpses in the hallway while I do the rest, and I'm a professional. Leaving dead bodies in plain sight is too risky, especially with the risk of those security cameras actually being monitored.

I head to the window, sliding it open to go onto the posh balcony, and the ledge I'm counting on is right there to the left. The wind up here is cold, and I let it bite into me. Distract me from the ridiculously long plunge below. One unexpected gust, and I'm a splatter on the street. I don't feel afraid, though. I never feel afraid.

I can't see the windows and balcony to the party's suite from here, I have to round the corner. But to get that far, I have about three dozen feet of clinging to the side of a skyscraper.

The key is to not think about it. As in all things, I let myself run on practiced instinct. Skills and methods honed through repetition.

The ledge holds as I creep my way along to that corner and peer around the edge.

It's all clear. And I carry on, winding about the corner of the building towards the first window. The curtains are shut still, thankfully, so that makes my job easier. Even assassins have to be grateful for small favors.

But then the doors to the balcony open, about a dozen feet away. So much for luck.

One of the security guards steps out, and I go still as a dead mouse. He looks around the cityscape and lingers a while, so my hand creeps down into my pocket, slowly— so slowly!—pulling the gun out, keeping it at the ready, aimed for him.

Time stands still, quiet but for the wind. There's about twenty stories between me and the ground. Long enough that if I fall, I'm going to have plenty of time to regret it. I focus my mind forward onto the man, let that cool calm grip my heart. My finger tenses on the trigger.

Then I hear him mutter seemingly to himself.

"Check in. All clear," he says into a headpiece that's all but invisible.

Now I have about five minutes, max. Then the next check-in will occur, and the men in the car would realize something's wrong, impeding my getaway.

The guard meanders a while longer before turning, heading back in, and shutting the door.

I lower my gun, slip it back into my pocket, and carry on, sidling along until I can climb up over the railing onto the balcony. I can peer in through the glass doors, into the hallway there. The suite beyond is massive, I know: I looked into it ahead of time. But the hallway is guarded by that lone security man.

Slipping the knife from my belt, I ever so carefully open the door, which I earlier jammed so that it never quite locks, though it appears to. The sounds of laughter and music from the partiers immediately fill my senses.

With smooth, quick motions, I simultaneously wrap my gloved hand around the guard's mouth and slide the blade into his back. I pierce his flesh right between his ribs, the long blade puncturing his heart then slicing through it and his lung.

He's dead, can barely even kick before it's all over. I don't take any time to revel in my victory. He's just one on a long list of guys who I've snuffed out. He wasn't even important enough for me to know his name.

I drag his body back out onto the balcony, wiping the blade off onto his blazer before I slip back inside. Time is of the essence now, the clock is ticking. But I can't hurry this, can't do anything more than carry on at my precise killing pace. If I rush, something will get fucked up, so even as I silently keep count of the seconds as they tick by, I stay calm and practiced.

Another guard walks into the hallway, rounding the corner, and I'm on him quick and smooth, hand over his mouth as my blade slices through his breast, ending his life. Ending lives is what I'm best at, and now I'm in my groove. It's not really a rush so much as an energy, feeding off these bastards' deaths.

Two guards down, four more to go.

I drag the body into the bathroom, stuffing him into the tub, pulling across the shower curtain. Before I can leave, one of the partygoers comes in. He's tipsy, doesn't notice me as I keep pressed to the wall behind a recess. He unzips, and I hear the sound of his pissing.

His life is ended in the blink of an eye. Never even had time to make peace with whatever god he prays to, poor sap. Not like a prayer would do guys like this any good.

Back in the hall, I head towards the private bedrooms.

A guard waits outside two of them, and there's no way I can approach him without him seeing me, so it's time for the gun.

One shot. A soft hiss of air. He's down, a hole in his forehead and a splatter of blood across the wall. It's messy. This is why I prefer the knife. I rush in to grasp his body before he can hit the ground. I jab the blade up into his skull from beneath his jaw anyhow, making sure it's done as I lower him down to the floor gently.

Then I listen at the doors.

One room is empty, the other, I hear two people inside. Sounds of moans, sex. They'll be distracted, making the kills even easier.

I head inside casually, the door opening to show them at the bed. One with his pants around his ankles, the other man on his knees. No sign of the woman.

I fire a shot and that ends the man's pleasure, but just as the other man realizes he's now fellating a corpse, I end him too. It worked well; neither got to cry out in the brief time it took me to kill them. Small favors.

I only have moments to get the rest of the job done. A bullet to the head is no absolute guarantee—people have lived through stranger things, and I make sure they're dead with my dagger once again before heading back out.

Nothing short of absolute success is acceptable to my employer. Nobody survives. That was the term of our contract. The stakes are too high for anything but.

Yet as I'm exiting the room, a guard arrives just in time to see the mess of his comrade splattered over the wall. That's why I hate guns. So messy. I can generally control the spurt of blood from my dagger until I'm done positioning the corpse.

Everything would go to hell here and now, if I weren't so well practiced at death. This is my life. I live it, breathe it. It's what I'm good at. Before he can utter a word, my hand is at his mouth, grasping tightly. He's reaching for the gun at his belt, but I stop him, seizing his hand.

The conundrum is that while I stopped him from sending warning to his fellow guards and getting his weapon, my two hands are now tied up as well.

He glares at me, a death stare. If looks could kill, he'd be as good an assassin as I am.

I let him push me back, though, and we're backpedaling into the gory murder scene of the bedroom. This guy's good. He's not distracted by the scene at all as I hoped he would be. Maybe he's born into death too. I have to up my game.

I head-butt him, and blood gushes from his nose. It's enough to set him off balance, so I twist around, get behind him, then force him to the floor. My two hands are still occupied, and I can't risk letting him speak or get his gun, so I make use of other limbs.

My legs get in around his neck, and I clench my thighs about him. I twist, using my hand at his mouth and my two legs to wrench his head back, suffocating him, straining that neck until at last... I hear it. The crack of bone.

His arms go limp, but he's not dead. There's still movement in his eyes. I've just crippled him, severed his spine. I end his misery with a knife at the back of his head, beneath his skull.

That's four guards down. And counting the two outside the door and the two at the car, that's all of them. But the job's far from done.

I head back into the hall, avoiding the main party room and its boisterous laughter and music. I go to the main door, open it up, and take out the two guards there. The blood spray spreads wide and won't be as easily noticed, so I haul them into the penthouse suite.

Now it's my time to join the party.

There's too many of them, even with how drunk and drugged they are. If I just walk in and start killing them, it'll be a noisy mess. So I go to a small, hidden fuse box in the wall. Something you'd never know was there unless you were an employee. I pry it open, cut the lights, and all is dark. But the music still plays.

I hear voices of surprise, laughter, mockery. Anger.

But the darkness is nothing to me. I switch on the night vision of my mask, but I don't really need it. I can still visualize them all where they were when the lights went out, pinpoint them by the sounds they each made. The guards took professionalism, skills, training to deal with. These rich and powerful men? They are like slaughtering hogs on the farm.

I walk in, and one by one, I began to end them. Grab, stab, slash. Grab, stab, slash.

It isn't until there are only three of them left that they even begin to notice the silence of their fellows. Another is dead before worry sets in.

"Stop fucking around, where'd you guys go?" asks one of the two remaining, flanking each side of the drugged woman, her body lewdly revealed and left splayed upon the sofa between them.

Before I can kill another, the man on the left turns on his phone's light, and it blinds me. But I don't need my eyes and pain is nothing that can distract me. With gun in one hand, I put a bullet through his head, and almost simultaneously, I lunge into the man on my right, the dagger jabbing up beneath his jaw and into his skull, crunching through cartilage as I kill them both.

They're dead. They're all dead, but for the guards at the car. And this lone woman.

The light from the phone is still surprisingly bright, and I turn off the night vision. I'm now able to see her laying there, chest heaving as she looks up at me, glassy eyed but aware.

I point the gun right to her forehead. I've done my mission so far with no more than a low gurgle of alarm. I've done it all with pure professionalism, and more than that, I've done it all happily. I've not regretted or failed to enjoy a single death tonight. And while I keep a stoic facade, all business, inside, my heart's racing with glee rather than anxiety.

No one lives. Or we're all fucked, rings Gregor's voice in my head.

What's one more, anyways?

CHAPTER 2

ALICIA

I awake to a pounding headache, something worse than I've ever experienced. No hangover has ever approached this nightmare in my skull, and I'm pretty much the queen of bad hangovers. The light that ekes through my eyelids is already too much, and I keep them shut as I clutch my forehead.

How much did I drink? I ask myself, confused.

But no amount of nursing my skull is gonna make things easier on me, so I force my eyes open. The sun streaming in through the window takes a while for me to get used to, stars appearing behind my eyes. Eventually, I adapt, and I realize that the curtains are drawn, and it's still a pain. The red drapes filter the light so that the Spartan, unfamiliar room is seemingly drowned in blood.

It reminds me of a nightmare I had the night before.

Me, lying there, blood spattering in the air as I watched some tall, dark, looming man pointing a gun at my head. He was like a specter of grim death. Stoic, towering, broad, and powerful. Hidden beneath dark clothes and a terrifying mask, blood soaking into his clothes.

A terrible dream, brought on by the drinking, I guess. Though I don't usually have nightmares.

The memory sends a shiver down my spine, doubly so as I try to understand my foreign surroundings. The cold concrete floors and brick walls, the simple bed that looks more like a cot.

What the hell happened last night?

I brush back my blonde hair, the strands still clinging to each other with leftover hairspray. My red dress is almost eerie in the strange light, and for a moment, for just a single moment, I wonder if I'm dead, surrounded in the color of blood.

I stand, my feet bare, my high heels tossed to the side. *I can't be dead,* I tell myself. *Dead people can't feel this damn hungover.*

Every beat of my heart sends a throbbing pain right to my temples, and I nearly stumble back to the bed, giving up in agony, but now I'm a bit curious. Did my boss take me somewhere?

"Hello?" I try to shout, but it comes out as a groggy murmur.

There's nothing, only eerie silence. The place is so still. The pain in my head seems to plead with me to relax and take my time, but the unfamiliar place urges me to get up and get out. So I head to the dark metal door of the room and try the handle. I fear that it's going to be locked, but a simple turn and it opens.

And more dreaded sunlight spills in. This time, it's unfiltered by curtains, and it's abrasive on my eyes. I feel like a vampire, or the walking dead.

"Where the hell am I?" I mutter, because last I remembered, I was with the congressman at some hoity-toity dinner. And this doesn't seem like the kind of place that my rich boss would've taken me. Even my place is less grey and unremarkable.

I step out into the room and slowly force my eyes to adjust. I can see a table, a kitchen, even a sofa. And while all of them are crisp and clean, they're once again simple. There's no real personality to the place at all, not even in a hotel kind of way.

"Sit," comes a deep, dark voice from right beside me. I didn't even see anyone there!

It's a lone man, broad in the shoulders, with sleek black hair brushed back. He sits in that grey metal chair by the small table, one other seat waiting for me. He's dressed darkly, a turtleneck and pants, both simple—clean, but definitely not a fashion statement. While his face… his face is chiseled, with a wide jaw and sharp, emerald eyes.

He's ominous, sure, but he's hot as hell. He's not cute, not like a guy my age. He's all man, but his seriousness gives me pause. I feel like I'm about to be chastised for something. Or hell, he can't be a cop, can he? I didn't do anything more than have a few drinks last night, I know that much. I might like to drink, but I never touch anything illegal, especially not out to dinner with my boss.

Immediately, it gets my back up, and I fold my arms across my chest. I must look silly with my messy hair and raccoon eyes, bare footed in a slinky mini-dress in the middle of the day.

"Where am I?" I ask, not sitting, because it's the only bit of rebellion I have. I don't deal well with authority figures, I guess you could say.

My first guess is that this is some security man left to watch over me by the congressman. It's the only thing I can think of that makes a lick of sense. Maybe there's been a national security threat and I've been taken to a secure bunker. Except I'm above ground, so that can't be it...

"You are at a safehouse," he explains to me, that husky voice curiously accented, but my mind's too fuzzy to work out exactly what kind of accent. Not that I'm any kind of expert. "Now sit," he says, uncrossing those thick, bulging arms from over his chest as he nudges a plate across the table toward my intended seating place.

It's a breakfast meal, hearty and much more than I'd ever eat. Eggs, ham, various veggies, toast. It doesn't exactly look fancy, but it looks healthy and recently prepared. "I'm not going to tell you again," he instructs me, and I finally stop fighting.

There's something about his tone that makes me want to obey. He's probably way out of my league, but with a guy as hot as him, I'm not about to piss him off. The chair is cold against my upper thighs, and the food both tempts me and makes me a little queasy.

"Where's Mr. Gallego?" I ask as I lift my fork, taking a bite first of the vegetables, since they seem the safest. And with how bland they are, I can't imagine they're going to upset my stomach. "I've never been in one of his safehouses before. I didn't even realize he had one."

The man gives me a stoic stare, his dark eyes piercing into me as he watches me eat. There's no answer at first—he simply stands up from his seat, and I catch a glimpse of just how towering he truly is. He's at least a foot and a half taller than me. Without a word, he goes to the kitchen, pours a glass of water, and returns, placing it beside my meal before reclaiming his seat.

"Do not worry about your employer," he instructs me in that dark tone of voice. "You won't be seeing him again any time soon."

That's... cryptic.

Though honestly, I can't really remember much about last night. We had our business dinner, and that was grand, but I definitely must have drank too much according to my hangover. I could swear I was only ordering wine. After all, I wanted to be on good behavior. I wanted Mr. Gallego to take me seriously, which is hard enough as a young blonde in New York.

I take another bite of food, mulling over what he's said.

"You're not the cops, are you? He's not in trouble, is he?"

He's a hard man to gauge, but when I ask if he's a cop I can see some slight betrayal of amusement upon his otherwise calm, chiseled facade. It sends butterflies into my stomach, and for a brief second, I wonder what he'd look like with an honest smile on his face. I bet he'd look sexy as hell.

"You worry a lot about others, for a woman I had to drag out, drugged and unconscious from a party of rich men," he says, his amusement dry. Really dry. If you could call it amusement at all.

But it makes him sound like a man who is tired of cleaning up other people's messes. Is this who the congressman calls when he's done something bad that needs covering up? Does that mean...

I nervously sit up, my hand running through my hair and getting caught in the tangled curls at the bottom.

"Wait, shit, am *I* in trouble? Did he say I did something wrong? Because I don't usually drink that much, I swear, and I don't even really remember what happened, so if he's afraid that I'm going to blab, I'm not going to. And I definitely didn't use any kind of drugs last night. Maybe it was just mixing the whites and reds."

His brows furrow, and he crosses those arms back over his chest, studying me with something between confusion and consternation. It gives me further opportunity to notice just how immaculate the man is. He's hard—hardened looking, to be exact—with dark stubble, a few faded scars upon his jaw, but his brows are so rigidly formed, eyebrows dark and naturally perfect. His eyes look almost kohl-lined. Overall, he's yummy, even if I am freaked.

"I got you out of there before they did anything to you," he says simply, but it's hard to tell if he's being honest or just feeding me the line he's supposed to.

"Oh." I take another bite of my food, the churning in my stomach not getting any better, but not getting any worse either. "Well, thank you," I say with a forced smile before glancing around at the barely furnished room. Whoever decorated has no sense of style. I tug up on the strap of my dress, feeling self-conscious. There's such a difference between being all dolled up at night and being dressed the same under the harsh light of day.

"Thank you for breakfast, too, I guess. My head is killing me." I take a sip of my water. "You got an Advil or something on you, Mr..."

Not eager to give his name, he reaches a hand down into his breast pocket and pulls out a pill, placing it on the edge of my plate. But aside from the fact I'm accepting some unknown drug from a stranger, I also notice for the first time that he has two holsters strapped beneath his bulky arms, attached to a dark leather harness that blends with his attire almost seamlessly.

"Mikhail," he says at last, after taking a moment to think it over. "What is your name?" he asks in return, but it's strange that he doesn't already know it, if he's working for Mr. Gallego.

What's happening in my life right now? The fact that he doesn't know my name or seem to even know Mr. Gallego... It's wrong. Something's fishy about this.

And worse, I can't seem to get that weird dream out of my head. I can even smell that weird scent that's completely unfamiliar to me, see the smoke rising from a gun.

"Why am I being held here?" I ask, ignoring his own request.

"For your own good," he says simply, darkly, that gaze of his unwavering. "Why were you with those men last night, Allie?" he says, apparently knowing my name after all. Or at least my nickname with friends.

"Who wouldn't go out for a free meal and drinks when their boss offers them the chance?" I say like it's the most obvious answer in the world, and it is. I have ambitions, after all, and sucking up to my boss might be the quickest way to success. They all think I'm just some dumb blonde, so I have to show them every chance I get that I'm not dumb, and I'm not even a real blonde.

Something about my answer seems to bother this strange man, Mikhail. His brows furrow.

"One of these men last night was your boss, Allie?" he asks, but that short-form of my name sounds so strange upon his accented voice. "Are you telling me they didn't just pick you up at some bar, ply you with drinks, and take you to their penthouse?"

"Ew, no. I'm not a *bar skank*," I say. "What's all this about, anyways? I'm already going to have to do damage control at the office if anyone finds out about this, so if we could just keep it quiet, I'd appreciate that, Mikhail." I give him a smile, my hand pushing out over top of the table, reaching out for his touch.

It's been a long time since I've found myself curious about a guy I just met, but Mikhail... he's definitely tall, dark, and handsome, and mysterious to boot. I wouldn't mind getting to know him better, see what makes him tick...

He studies me a while with that penetrating gaze of his, the kind of look that makes me feel naked, and not just because I'm still wearing the slinky dress from last night. No, this is a powerful man who can see right through me, to the depths of my being. All the questions? It's like he knows the answers to them all but is just confirming them. Sometimes because they're too ludicrous for him to buy at face value, other times because he just wants to be absolutely certain.

"How many people at the office know you went out with your boss last night?" he asks me, his voice getting even grimmer, more serious.

"A few... We left right from the office, and then he took me to my place to get changed. I mean, it was just whoever was working late on a Friday night. Well, and his secretary, because I'm pretty sure she knows everything."

The answer doesn't surprise him, as I knew it wouldn't, but it troubles him. That much is clear.

He lifts an arm, runs his hand back over his sleek, dark hair and casts his gaze down to my food, still not finished.

"Eat up. You will need all you can get. You were out for a very long time, thanks to what they slipped you. And if you don't eat, the nausea you feel now will be nothing compared to what's to come," he explains casually, standing up from the table again, looming over me.

What have they slipped me?

"Mr. Gallego wouldn't give me anything like that. He's a congressman, for Pete's sake. Could you imagine the scandal if I was drugged while on a business meeting? The press would never let him live that down."

"Eat," he orders me sternly. "You are going to need your strength, and there won't be much else to do around here for the next few days at least," he instructs as he glares down at me, those large, powerful hands upon his hips.

Next few days?!

Instead of eating, I stand up from my chair, thinking for a brief second that if I stand up I'll feel more powerful. I apparently forgot that I barely come up to his pecs, am at most half his weight, and my glare is probably not going to cow him the way I hope it will. Not to mention the fact that I'm not too steady on my feet right now.

Still, a girl's gotta try, right?

"A few days? Listen, I can't stay here a few days. Firstly, I have a job to get to, and that... that... *cot* you gave me might work for a drunk tank, but I'm sober now and that's not going to cut it. And lastly," I say, having lost count of my points, "I'm supposed to be helping Mr. Gallego on his re-election campaign this weekend. That was why he invited me out, to give me more details on what he needed me to do."

As expected, my resistance proves absolutely useless upon him. I might as well have just blown sparkles at him for all he seems swayed by my words.

"None of that matters anymore," he states simply in that harsh accent of his. "You have no job to return to. Gallego will not be running for re-election. And you are going to sit down, eat your food, then get changed, curl up on the couch, and watch some TV," he instructs me. And a quick glance shows me that the drab couch indeed sits before a rather unimpressive flat screen TV I hadn't even noticed before now.

"I suggest you get used to your accommodations, Ms. Allie," he says firmly. "For your own safety, you are staying here for the time being."

This is when dread really starts creeping in.

"What... what happened last night?" I ask, my hands suddenly turned to ice and beginning to tremble.

"Nothing that should concern you any longer if you care for your life," he says to me with stern seriousness. "Now eat. Get comfortable. You are here until it becomes safe for you to leave again. For your own benefit I suggest you get used to it," he explains before strolling past the couch.

There, he leans down and lifts a pile of clothes from the sofa, resting it on the back of the couch and patting it. It's a pink, girly color.

"Here is a change of clothes for you. There is food in the kitchen, the TV has cable, and the bathroom is right there," he explains, pointing to a small door off to the side.

"I will be back later," he adds as he heads to the main door.

"Wait!" The fear of being alone and not knowing what happened is apparently way stronger than my fear of what actually happened last night. Who is he?

"Just tell me what happened at the party," I plead, my head getting woozy and sending me off balance as I careen into the couch.

It's all hazy, but I think he catches me, sweeping in faster than my eyes can see. But then it's all darkness.

I HAVE no idea how long I was out, but as I come to I see the light streaming in through the window, a mesh of protective bars filtering it only a little. I realize I'm on that plain, grey sofa in front of the TV and window, still locked in the drab room.

More urgently, however, I feel something else come over me: imminent nausea.

The dark stranger, Mikhail, had warned me, but when it hits… it hits like a ton of bricks. I'm already on my side, but I lunge for the edge of the sofa to hurl, and thankfully, find there's already a bucket waiting for me in place.

This isn't a hangover. This is something more vile and scary, and I'm starting to believe the man when he said I was drugged. It's almost impossible for me to believe, though. I'm just some aide for the congressman, trying to get some experience and work my way through school. Being drugged is something I'd more easily have accepted if I was out with guys my own age.

A sense of betrayal comes over me, fear over what my employer was intending on doing to me. If Mikhail is to be trusted—and I don't know if he can—then he saved me from something terrible. It doesn't take a lot of imagination to wonder what a group of men would have done to a drugged and helpless young woman.

The pain that shoots through my stomach sends tears to my eyes, and my entire body feels overheated with anxiety. When finally I'm emptied of every last bit of food, there's still a lingering agony in my gut, but my nausea subsides.

I'm still in my crumpled dress from the night before... was it last night? I have no idea of the time, I realize, only that it's sunny outside. The window faces a drab building across the street, completely unremarkable and unmarked, for that matter.

I grab some of the paper towel next to the sofa and wipe off my mouth before I stumble to the bathroom. Or try to, at least. My legs are weaker than I could've imagined, and I feel so dizzy. It takes me a while to make my way there. The washroom has the same kind of austere layout as the rest of the 'safehouse.' But it's clean enough to eat off of, and that's comforting enough.

I vomit again, but it's really more of a dry heave, since I have no more food to leave me. I notice a toothbrush and paste there, so I clean my mouth out once I'm done, trying to get the sickening tang of my own vomit out of there.

One look in the mirror, and I'm instantly feeling awful again. I'm pale, my makeup is smudged, and I look like hell. No wonder Mikhail didn't look the least bit interested in me. Well, that and the fact that I'm technically his captive, I suppose.

He said he wants to keep me safe, though. Safe from what?

I wash away the streaked eyeliner and smudged lipstick, and that gets rid of some of my disaster-case appearance.

My hair feels awful, but at least the hairspray kept in my curls. Still, I desperately need a shower.

I shut and lock the door, quickly stripping out of my dress and turning the shower on hot. Steam fills the small room, and it would be soothing if I didn't feel so troubled. My stomach churns, and not just because of whatever they slipped me last night.

It's all just darkness, and when I step into the shower and the hot water hits me, so too does a sob. What happened last night? I want to scream at the fact that I can't remember, that I don't know what happened. How does someone just lose hours of their life? I've been drunk before, but never forgotten so much like this.

The cascade of water does little to soothe my troubled mind, and tears mingle with the shower. I feel like screaming, like crying, like giving up. I'm terrified, and don't know what's happening. It didn't even occur to me to check my phone. Maybe someone's messaged me, given me some words of helpful comfort.

I quickly finish the shower, feeling a little more like myself before wrapping myself in the towel and padding out towards the bedroom. I check my shoes and around the cot, but there's nothing. No phone.

Fuck, that must be how he found out my name! I curse myself for not having figured it out sooner. Of course he stole my phone. Why wouldn't he, if I was being held captive?

For my own good, he'd said. Well, *I* should be the one to decide that. He can't just come into my life, kidnap me, then tell me it's for my own good.

I grab the clothes he set out for me and quickly pull them on. Shocker, they fit. This guy is even more of a creep than I figured! Anger starts fueling me. I'm not going to sit here like some helpless damsel. I'm going to get out.

I go to the barred window, finding myself several stories up and without a fire escape. That's gotta be against the law, but so is kidnapping, so whatever. I try to open it, but it seems like it's sealed shut, and I let out a groan.

A wave of exhaustion hits me, and I have to lean against the wall for support.

What if he's watching? What if there are cameras? I shake the thought away. It's not going to do me any good to think like that. I just have to get out and find out what's going on.

I try the front door, but it's locked and made of metal. There's no budging it. Then I go to the kitchen, where I find there are no knives and one locked cupboard, but I do get a thick spoon and take it to the window. I try to push it in, see if maybe I can't pry the window from its setting, but I'm weak and having little success.

I must be at it for a while, because I eventually get so exhausted I slump to my knees in that pink set of around-the-house wear. What is it he's gotten me, anyhow? Yoga pants, socks and a shirt. It's deranged, I feel like a girl in my father's home again, and the helplessness makes me want to sob.

"The window is sealed shut," comes his dark voice, standing behind the sofa, and I cry out, startled. I didn't hear him come in at all! And it's not like my trying to pry open the window was a noisy affair!

I scramble backwards, away from his towering form. The daze must have parted, though, because earlier I thought he was cute, but now...

I'm being held captive by an Adonis. He's all muscle and smoldering glare.

Just what I need.

"You shouldn't sneak up on a girl! What if I'd been changing?"

"You would change in the living room when I gave you a bedroom all your own?" he asks in that thickly accented voice, which I'm starting to realize sounds vaguely eastern European. But he's got his brow raised to me in challenge as he stands there, looming, larger than life, waiting for my response as he holds a small cloth bag.

"Well, maybe," I say defiantly, though even I can tell I sound more like a petulant child than a grown woman. I glance down at the bag, my arms folded beneath my chest. "What's that?"

He gives the bag a toss onto the sofa.

"It's medicine for nausea. It will help you keep your food down," he explains to me, the towering brute looking exactly as I'd seen him last, except he must have shaved away the stubble in the interim. But it's quickly regrowing. "Plus some magazines for entertainment," he adds, as if this is the 1990s and people still read magazines.

"And my cellphone?"

"I had to destroy it," he says casually.

"What?" That was pretty much the last thing I expected him to say, and I take a step towards him angrily. "But it has all my contacts!"

"It could also be used to track you down. Is a phone worth your life?" he asks me pointedly, and I'm starting to hate his chiseled face and eerie calm. He radiates confidence and power, like some smug son of a bitch who's never been knocked down a peg in his life.

I'm aghast. I can't believe it. My phone. The newest model that I had to shell out a ridiculous sum for after waiting in line…destroyed. By this *thug*.

"How *could* you?!" I demand, rising up onto my knees and glaring at him. "Do you have any idea what that thing meant to me?"

He takes his time, undaunted, those dusky eyes looking me over as if I'm a strange, even repulsive creature. "More than your life, it seems," he says simply before turning to leave.

But I can't let him leave, and I lunge over the back of the sofa to grab his arm at the wrist.

"No, wait!" I insist, but even I realize that it's only by choice that he stops. That thick arm beneath my hands is a thickly corded knot of muscle, and he could yank me over the back of that sofa with ease.

"What?" he asks dryly, looking back and down at me. And though he acts so calm, I get the impression I am pushing his patience to the limit.

Even though I'm pissed, I don't want to be alone again. I'm terrified, and having him near me is safer, somehow, even if he is my captor. I hate the waiting, because when he's gone, my head goes back to what might have happened last night.

What *really* happened.

And I know now that he's definitely got me locked up

in here good, and by the looks of things, he's keeping me a while.

I let go of his thick wrist and take in a deep breath.

"How long are you going to keep me locked up?"

That question seems to take him by surprise, because he doesn't answer me right away. He takes a moment. And that more than anything else about my capture worries me.

"I don't know yet," he says in that gruff voice of his. "I have to see how long the search for you persists. If I let you go too soon, then it's just as well I didn't haul you out at all. I should just as well have put a bullet in your head then and there that night."

His ominous words make me tremble, all the more because I see the handle of his gun sticking out from behind his back as he faces me, side-on.

There's some part of me, some part I'm not ready to reconcile with, that knows that what happened that night wasn't just a nightmare. Waking up and wondering if I was dead was natural, because I remember a pistol pointed at my head.

I almost died.

This man almost killed me.

It makes me almost throw up, my stomach churning in disgust and terror, but I swallow it all down. I can't blow this. I can't give him a reason to kill me. I ignore the burning behind my eyeballs, the frightened tears that want to spill but I won't allow.

Swallowing back the bile and the lump in my throat, I return my eyes to his.

"Mikhail," I say, trying to build a bit of a repertoire with him. That's what they always say on TV, right? Make your kidnapper get to know you. But he already knows me, at least in part... It's still worth a shot. "I'm scared."

His eyes narrow as he stares at me, into me. And he's studying me. I worry that my attempt to sway him failed, but then it happens: he softens. Those broad shoulders lower a little, his sweater hugging those thick muscles showing the tension melt a little throughout him. He might be a scary boogeyman of death, but he's still susceptible to a girl's charms.

"You have no need to be scared while you are here, Allie. It is what's on the other side of that window," he says, jabbing a finger at it pointedly, "that you must fear. And if you keep that in mind, you will be fine."

He says it all so seriously I could almost be convinced, if it weren't for the fact I am fairly certain this man is a murderer.

But I give him a small nod, like I'm on his side. As if we both want the same thing. And, if he does want me to be safe, then we definitely want the same thing.

"I get that, but Mikhail, people are going to be looking for me. And my mom, she's... I mean, a few years ago, she had a fall, and it affected her mind. Dad passed years ago, and she really needs me to help take care of her."

His brow furrows just a bit, and he's silent again. I know I have him considering my words. He takes his time and wets his lips, and I feel like I have him.

"If you die, your mother would be very put out then, *nyet*?" he says, that strange words on the end completely foreign to my ears.

"She needs me, so I can't die," I say, trying to choose my words carefully, even though I'm panicking that he's going to leave and I'm going to be stuck. He can't leave!

"But she has pills. Medication she has to take, and I have to make sure she takes it and gets to all of her appointments. I don't even know what day it is..."

He pauses a moment, but then reaches into his back pocket, pulling out a small pad of paper and a pencil the length of my thumb. He puts it down right in front of me.

"Write out the details of your mother's care," he instructs me very pointedly, his gaze narrowing. I feel like I'm under a heat lamp as a detective scrutinizes me.

My shoulders slump, and I sit down on the couch, pencil in hand as I try to remember everything that was in my phone. It's pretty sad that I can barely remember, considering how routine it is.

I scribble down as I remember.

Every third Tuesday, appointment with Dr. Nevaro.

Twice daily reminders to take her pills. Blue in the morning, yellow and white at night before bed.

Once a month, hospital for treatment for osteoporosis.

I hand it back to him.

"I don't know how to spell all the drug names, but she has real problems with me not being around. I really need to check on her, Mikhail. You have a mom, right? And she means a lot to you?"

He takes the paper from me and sizes it up before folding it and slipping it into his pocket.

"My mother is long dead," he says grimly as he turns and walks away. My heart sinks.

But as he reaches the door he pulls it open and stops, looking back me.

"I will see yours doesn't yet meet the same end," he states simply, then swiftly vanishes out the door, leaving me to the simple furnishings, all by myself.

"Fuck!" I cry out into my humble cage. I can't stay here. I don't care how safe he thinks it is, I can take care of myself, and being held captive by a man I don't know—a man who openly carries a gun on his hip—is not going to work for me.

He said the window was sealed shut, but there's gotta be a way out.

Then I remember my stilettos. Maybe I could use those to bust open the glass! Or hammer the door.

No matter what, I'm getting out of this safehouse-turned-prison.

CHAPTER 3

MIKHAIL

Every meeting with that girl is a struggle.

If she's not taunting me with her natural good looks, she's tugging at heartstrings I didn't even know I had. It's a fucking nuisance.

I pull on my leather jacket, make the phone call I have to, then head right out. But now I'm here, back at this dark, dingy bar. Where low life mobsters come to get work. I hate this place and almost never come. The work finds me at this point in my career, after all.

Smoking laws forbid it, but the law has no consequence in this place, so smoke lingers in the air as a bunch of guys, young and old, try and put on airs of being tough. But every single one of them is shaken by my entry.

Every one of them knows who I am, by reputation or rumor.

I could rule them. I could be boss of this whole stretch of the city if I wanted to.

But I turned that down long ago. I'm happiest doing what I do.

"Mikhail," says Nikita behind the bar, the surprise on her face mixed with pleasure. She's a good girl, the only good part about this dive. "Didn't expect you here!" she says as she pulls out a glass and starts to make me a drink without even asking. She knows what I like, even now.

"I was in the neighborhood," I say with a shrug of my shoulders, leaning in over the bar and shooting the young punk nearest me a look.

He scurries off, taking his drink further down the bar and giving me the space I want.

"Well, I'm just happy to see you," Nikita says, pouring me up a vodka and cranberry, even adding a little slice of lime. That's new. "Not many pleasant faces around here," she adds, and I know it. These men have no concern for women like her—they're just cargo or commerce, to be used up until worthless.

I try the drink, and to my surprise I like it, that lime adding a touch of something I didn't know I was missing.

"Truth be told, Nikki," I say, leaning in, speaking to her in confidence, "I am curious as to the word on my latest job."

She arches a brow at me, looking truly surprised.

"That's not like you, Mikhail," she says, putting the vodka bottle back. And I note it's even the kind I like. Russian Standard, straight from home. Nothing's quite as smooth as it. She's so damned considerate of me, like a little sister I never had.

"This is a… special case," I say simply. "A very big job. Wondering what the word on it around town is."

"You always get the big ones," she says, leaning in closer herself, talking quietly. "Not much is being said. More hush-hush than usual. So it must've been very important," she says, searching my eyes for an answer, but I give none. No flicker in my face to betray an ounce of info.

"So nothing, then?" I ask to confirm, but she licks her lips and peers down, thoughtfully.

"I overheard some of the guys talking earlier," she says softly to me. "Word from a crooked cop was that security cameras showed a witness to a big hit was unaccounted for. They are looking for her."

Fuck.

"How recent was this?" I ask, trying not to betray my urgency. But she can pick up on it, I think.

"Just about forty minutes ago," she says, and she reaches beneath the bar, taking out the vodka again and pouring me a straight shot. "Very fresh news, they're putting out the word now."

"There a description of the girl?" I ask, then down the vodka she poured me in one smooth motion.

"Vasili," she says, pointing her chin towards the weasley man. "He has some info on her, I believe. They're looking into things now."

"Thanks, Nikki," I say, sliding a hundred dollar bill across the bar to her. Her eyes widen and she looks to me.

"If I hear anything more, I'll let you know," she says, and I nod.

"I know you will. Stay safe, little one," and she rolls her eyes at me, being far from little. She is 5'8" and a grown woman, after all. But I still saw her as the famished, undernourished girl they hauled out of the dockyards.

I turn to leave, but then in through the front doors comes the boss. The *Avtoritet.*

He's escorted on both sides by two young brutes he

trusts, and while the sneer he holds makes it look like he's ready to make every occupant of the bar feel like shit, his gaze settles on me. And I steal some of the thunder from his entry.

"Volkov," he says, using my last name, and I know he's struggling on how to handle my presence. I never come around, which makes things easier for him. Seeing as I was the guy who passed up his position. The guy who had every right to be over him, but was only technically under his authority.

It's an awkward situation for him, I admit.

"Gregorovich," I say with a simple nod in return, which is more than the vile shit deserves from me. I loathe this man, not just for what he's done, but for how he gives me so few things to insult him about. He's not fat, he's not ugly; he's just a manipulative bastard who plays things cautiously all the time. Too cautious. Cautious to the point of paranoia.

Which would all be excusable, except he's also greedy.

And a greedy, paranoid mafia boss is a dangerous thing for everyone.

"How nice of you to pay us a visit," he says, tugging open his thick overcoat as Nikita rushes around to help him out of it. "I trust everything is alright?" And with that brow arched at me, I know I have already engaged more of his suspicion than I wish to.

"Just visiting an old friend," I say, giving a light smile to Nikita, which she bashfully returns. I don't generally let slip any emotion around these men, but it's important they know who I favor, so they know better than to mess with her.

"I see," Gregorovich says, looking me over once more

than Nikita as well. "Well it's fortunate timing, there's a matter we can discuss. In back," he says, leading the way. It's the most presumptuous thing he's yet dared do with me in front of others.

Surprisingly, however, along the way he gestures for Vasili to follow. He's a two-bit crook, and why he's being trusted with anything baffles me.

But I have a sinking suspicion this is about the matter I came here for, so I follow after, into the back room, with its reinforced walls. It's empty but for a simple metal table with some chairs, and he helps himself to a spot there while one of his men pats down the underside of the table, checking for any listening devices.

I stand back, fold my arms as another of the guards pats down Vasili as well, checking him over. Gregorovich trusts no one.

When they come to me I don't budge, and they back off, knowing better.

"What is the issue at hand?" I ask brusquely.

"You fucked up," Vasili says with malicious glee, but I don't so much as grace him with a glance.

Gregorovich clears his throat, cutting off Vasili, preening at his expensive suit. I leave him the dubious honor of being the only one sitting.

"There are some loose ends from your job," Gregorovich says.

"I do not leave loose ends," I say firmly, an edge to my voice to let them know I'm serious. But I want more info, so I'm careful not to be too rough with them.

"Well, this time, the police think you have," Gregorovich responds carefully. "And they're looking for a potential witness seen entering the hotel with the party."

"That no-women no-kids rule of yours has finally fucked you up, Volkov," Vasili says with sneering relish, fidgeting a lot. Probably because he's constantly wired on a cocktail of different drugs.

"Was there a woman there when you did the job?" Gregorovich asks calmly, and I know it won't be easy to lie to him. He's perceptive, for a greedy little shit.

"I agreed to take on this job, knowing it might lead to a bad place," I say firmly. "But I did the job, and no one survived."

"Then how do you explain this?" Vasili says, pulling out the picture of Allie with the men I'd slain. It's not great quality, clearly taken from a security camera. But it's her. I take a moment to soak it in before Vasili gets into my face, that greasy weasel so full of himself.

I take a moment to slam my fist into his throat and send him choking and sputtering back against the wall.

"Why is this little rat fuck in here with us?" I ask Gregorovich pointedly.

"I've tasked him with finding this woman. And making sure she can't talk," he replies, ignoring the coughing and cursing of Vasili as we engage.

"She has nothing to tell anyone," I insist calmly, not overplaying the point. I can't give him reason to suspect me. "I did a clear sweep. Every single person in there when I did my hit died by my hand. And when I was done, I double-checked. Triple-checked. And calmly walked out."

Vasili is gasping for air, making a noisy distraction.

"Then there is nothing to worry about, and this is just an added precaution," Gregorovich assures me with a placid, fake smile.

"Too many added precautions can land one in trouble with the feds," I say, knowing to add anymore would let him find me out. "But do as you need. My work is done." I turn to leave, but one of the guards is in my way, and I have to stare him down.

Which gives Vasili enough time to choke out a few words.

"When I find that girl, I'm gonna cut her into ribbons. She'll be more useless to the cops than a shredded document," Vasili says, and my fists clench, my jaw tightening.

I turn my head slowly, stare down that weasel shit.

"Everyone knows what it is you like to do with women, *govnjúk*. But if I catch you laying a hand on one," and I walk over to him, making him back against the wall as I stare down at him, "the only ribbon you'll be worried about getting cut is the one between your legs."

I don't give him time to snark back, I just plant my knee into his groin and make it so that he won't think about women for a few days without a lot of pain.

"You should not trust this little *govnjúk*, he'll land you in trouble someday," I caution Gregorovich before I just walk out, knowing I was in a precarious position and might've just overplayed my hand.

CHAPTER 4

ALICIA

This safehouse wasn't set up to keep people in, it was set up to keep people out, and that's my one advantage here. But so far it's not really paying off for me very well.

My high heel didn't turn out to be the miracle tool I'd hoped it would, and my attempts to use it to pry open the door or barred windows failed. The utensils in the kitchen were all even worse, plastic and easily broken.

On the plus side, I didn't find any cameras, so maybe it was just a fluke earlier when he came in just as I was trying to bust out. I still don't know what to make of him. Part of me believes him that he only wants to keep me safe from whatever the hell happened that night. But I don't know if that's just lust speaking or not. He's the hottest guy I've ever seen, and there's nothing more that I'd want to believe than the idea that he's my Prince Charming, rescuing me from some bad men.

As I exhaust all the options I can think of, though, it's seeming less and less likely that escape is possible. I've not heard or seen anyone else, and I still have no idea how much time has passed since that man captured me.

Rescued.

Who knows.

The only thing I do know is that my window is my best option for escape, and I can't give up. I glance around the room, and when my eyes settle on the TV, I get a bright idea. It's big, and probably too much to carry comfortably, but maybe if I can hoist it up and throw it through the glass...

It's a long shot. A really long shot. And I don't know what I'm going to do once the window is out, but I can't just sit here like a damsel in distress for Mikhail to *save* me from whatever is happening out there. I have to rescue myself, damn it!

I unplug the TV and try to pick it up, but it digs into my arms, almost too big for me to lift, but finally I manage.

It's a struggle to heave the TV, but as I heft it up, I hear the doorknob turn, and as I struggle to put the TV back into place, I realize there's no way I'm doing that before he catches me.

"What are you doing?" he asks, that deep, dark voice of his so blasé about the whole thing as he stands there watching me. "If you didn't like the placement of the TV, you could have just asked," he says, the grizzled man seeming almost amused by me, if I could read anything on his stoic face.

I brush some hair from my eyes, feeling guilty as sin, as if I'm doing something wrong by trying to break out of this prison. I'm scared, and I don't want to piss him off, but at the same time, I'm curious about him. About who he actually is.

I've gotta get a grip.

"Yeah, well, I never got your number," I answer back, filled with snark.

"My apologies," he says dryly, and he heads into the kitchen area, toting a large brown paper bag that looks to be packed with boxes. He returns a moment later, the towering brute plucking the TV from my grasp and putting it back where it came from. "You know, smashing out the window would not help you. It is barred, and the streets are many floors below. Nobody could hear your cries," he explains to me with the air of a patient, wiser man, even if he has the look of someone dangerous in that tight-fitting sweater and jeans.

"At least I'd be able to enjoy some fresh air," I say, my arms folded beneath my chest, but it's all bravado. I feel like a quivering bird held in his palm, just waiting for him to squeeze a little too hard. I'm only alive because of him, or so he says, but this isn't my life or the life I ever wanted.

He walks past me over by the wall and taps a thermostat there.

"You can control AC and heat here, and don't worry about the light bill," he says with a hint of humor to his voice before he heads back into the kitchen.

"Ahh, funny," I say, some of my normally sarcastic self seeping out. I like it when he banters with me.

I have to walk around the sofa to see him there, taking out plates and serving up some food from the packages he brought. Some take-out, no doubt.

My stomach growls with desire. Since whatever drugs I had made me reject everything in my system, I've been starving and too afraid to eat. I sniff the air, catching the various scents of foreign cuisine, and my palm goes to my tummy to quiet it down. Last thing I need is for this guy to know how desperate I am for a bite.

"I couldn't dream of putting you out with an exorbitant bill, though," I say, trying to keep things light. Maybe that's what is needed.

"So considerate." I notice he's serving up egg rolls, and that familiar scent comes back to me: Chinese food. "I did not catch any dietary concerns," he says with that accent of his, "but I figured everyone likes Chinese."

He comes out of the kitchen, laying the two paper plates full of food onto the table before retreating back in to pour us both up some water.

I stare after him in disbelief.

"A meal together. How cute," I grin, but before he's even returned from the kitchen, I've scalded my tongue on the egg roll, and I'm grabbing for the glass of water like a toddler.

So much for playing it cool.

"It is still very fresh," he says, a caution that comes too late. "They know me there, make it just for me. But this time I had them prepare a little extra," he gestures to one side of my plate. "You're a lovely young woman, so I thought perhaps you are a vegetarian or some such, everything on this side is free of meat," he explains before seating himself down like he was in a mess hall and digging his fork into a piece of meat.

He's no vegetarian, that's for sure.

I gulp back the water, but I can already tell I won't be able to taste anything else on my plate with a burned tongue, and I sigh.

"So you're vying for, like, the most considerate kidnapper award?"

"When one does something, you must always give it your best," he says in that odd way of his, drawing out the words with that eastern flavor, and a healthy dose of dry, dark humor. Though the close proximity gives me time to study him, to see the scar on his face, right up along the highest part of his cheekbone, his jawline lightly stubbled with dark hair.

He catches me staring, and I quickly avert my eyes. I've never been the kind of girl who's been shy around men, but there's something about him that makes me feel like a girl again. If I wasn't his captive, I'd probably have hit on him at a bar or something. He has a rugged charm about him, and I admit that his sense of humor aligns with mine a little too well.

"So you're single, huh?" I venture a guess, though as soon as the words are out, I wish I hadn't said them.

He arches a brow, looking about as surprised by the question as I am, but nods his head.

"*Da,*" he says, and I know enough from movies to realize that means 'yes.' "A man in my line of work doesn't make a good husband. A woman deserves more than a man who is out at all hours, life on the line all the time." He shakes his head slowly as he eats, "No. I tried that long ago, before I entered the Special Forces."

"Military?" I ask, surprised he's even answering any of my questions. I take a bite of something I don't have a name for, but mostly I'm finding myself curious. He hasn't actually hurt me or put me in any danger, though I know better than to trust him. At least, my brain knows. The rest of my body wants to take in everything he tells me.

"*Spetsnaz,*" he says, nodding his head before downing almost his entire glass of water in a few gulps. "We were like your Navy Seals in a way," he says, those dark eyes of his searching out mine as he explains things to me like a patient teacher. "We went where soldiers know better than to go. Did things they could not. You understand?" he asks, and he's waiting. Watching. Wanting to know if I truly do understand.

Is it meant to be taken as a threat?

I try not to flinch under his hard stare, and suck in a deep breath. I will not let this man intimidate me.

"You're a badass. I get it."

"So you should understand that you're safer here with me than on your own out there," he says, speaking calmly as he points to the door. "There are men after you as we speak. I have confirmed it for myself."

"Listen, I might be cute, but I'm not so cute that anyone's going to be after me," I say, masking my fear with sarcastic humor. I don't know if he's really being serious, but something in his eyes tell me he is. But I can't just hide in here the rest of my life.

He laughs at me just a little and continues to eat a moment before speaking.

"By no fault of your own, you have been a part of something ugly. I wish it was not so, but I can't change what's already done. Your boss is dead," he says, the proclamation rather brusque and pointed. "A man like him simply doesn't die and go unnoticed, *nyet*? And it is too important to leave open to question. The kind of questions a surviving witness can raise."

"I didn't *witness* anything!"

"It does not matter," he says, and I see his thick forearm swell through his sweater as he clenches his fist. "It only matters what they think you witnessed," he explains to me, his voice getting darker, more serious. "Do you think someone has a congressman killed without wanting to make very sure it never comes back to him, hmm?" he says, his eyes boring into me with their intensity.

It sends a shiver down my spine, and I swallow hard.

"I can't stay here forever. What are you going to do to me?"

"To you?" he asks, eyes wide before he laughs and looks away. "Nothing. But I do not send pretty, young women to their deaths. No matter how dense in the head they're being," he adds, that patience eked away a little as he puffs up his broad chest and sighs.

"I'm not dense. But how many kidnapped women have you *saved* that are just totally fine with being your captive, huh?"

He gives a light, exasperated sigh and finishes off another generous bite before looking back at me.

"I do not make a habit of this, if it's what you're meaning. You are the first. But too much time and money had been sunk into getting the target where he was needed to be. If I didn't do the job then, a messier hit would've happened as they all left, and you'd be dead instead of complaining," he says, revealing all that info so calmly.

A storm is brewing within me, emotions surfacing that I didn't know even lingered beneath my skin. My heart pounds, and I stare at the man ahead of me. I know what he meant about what he did. He killed people. He still does.

I'm here, having a quaint little dinner with what is possibly the sexiest killer in the world. Not that I know a lot of killers. Any, actually, before him.

My skin flushes, and for a second, I feel like I'm going to be sick again, but I swallow it back as I force myself to stand. Tears are stinging my eyes, but I blink them away, fury and terror swirling within me.

"You want me to thank you or something, Mikhail? Is that what this whole dinner business is about?"

He takes one of the napkins in hand, unfurls it, and calmly wipes his mouth.

"I do not want your thanks or your gratitude," he says, still sitting there at the table. "What I want is for you to sit tight until it is safe for you to go. Or until I figure out where you can go that won't get you killed," he says, looking right at me with those dark eyes of his.

The eyes of a murderer.

He should make me sick. He *does* make me sick. So why am I so drawn to him, and what does that say about me? Normal girls don't feel drawn to their murdering kidnapper.

I take in another deep breath of air as I continue to stare at him.

"I'm not staying here. If you were supposed to kill me and you didn't, they're going to be looking at where you led them. It's only a matter of time before they find this place, if they don't already know of it."

I have no idea who *they* are, or if I'm correct, but I'm taking a giant stab in the dark in order to gain my freedom. To plead with him for a way out.

His brows furrow a little, and he looks at me.

"Only a handful of men in this city know who did the hit. You're sitting with one. The others are all well under my influence," he says with that stoic gaze of his, unflinching and serious. "And furthermore, they do not know about this place. This is my safe house. A place where nobody in my life knows how to get to. Where if everyone in the world turned on me, I could come here and last out a long, long wait. This place," he says, jabbing his long index finger into the table, "is my insurance. And now, it is yours."

I hate that somehow, he's making me feel bad for taking this all for granted, and I fidget under his hard stare.

"People... people who hire hitmen don't just forget about murder witnesses. I've seen the movies, you know. The ones where people are sitting and having breakfast twenty years after the fact, and they get a gun in their face. This is never going to leave me."

His broad jaw sets tight, and he looks at the food, taking a deep breath.

"I've told them that there were no witnesses. That you must have left the scene before I hit. The local boss is paranoid and wants to take you out just in case," he explains, turning his gaze towards me, staring hard. "But when you don't show up for a while, and nothing comes of it...you will be forgotten. Business moves on, as usual. As it must," he explains firmly.

I shift forward. This is dumb. I shouldn't be getting closer to him. I shouldn't be placing my hand on his jaw, my fingers caressing him tenderly.

And the worst part is I don't even know if it's all just a ploy to get him to let me go or if I just want to touch him. To know he's real, to feel that stubble beneath my palm.

"You're trying to do the right thing," I say more softly, and I truly believe that's what he thinks he's doing. Hell, maybe that is what he's doing. Maybe, beneath that gruff exterior and hard gaze and that gun on his hip, he really is my knight in shining armor.

My fingers trace back over his jaw towards that red scar on his face, and I watch as his rugged features contort into a look of curiosity. He's almost as confused by my actions as I am.

"I am not a school boy to be manipulated," he says, his voice a little quieter. "I am looking after you, not because I'm out to be the hero. Not because I expect some big thank-you." He reaches up and wraps his hand about my wrist, that grasp of his so tight as he rises up to tower over me again. "I saved you because I wanted to. I'll keep you alive because that's my desire. It is no more complicated than that, and I expect nothing else than for this to end with you alive and well, if cranky."

My breathing quickens despite myself as my gaze is forced upwards. He's just a hair's breadth away from me, and if I leaned forward just a little, my chest would be pressed against his abs. It's tempting, for all the wrong reasons.

"Why did you want to save me?" I ask, surprised at how quiet and shaky my voice has become.

He's still holding my hand, and though I can no longer touch his jaw where he keeps it, I could reach out, touch that broad, hard chest of his if I wanted. If I wasn't quaking before the towering Russian.

But that question seems to stump him a little, or maybe he's just not sure if he wants to be honest, because he doesn't answer right away.

"Because I chose to, that's all there is to it," he says, releasing my arm. But even this stoic brute doesn't do a good job of hiding the truth this time, because I can tell there's more.

It hangs between us, but I don't push. Not this time. Not if I hope to see him let me go from my prison cell.

And do what? That voice in the back of my mind nags at me. I want to be free just because I don't like being trapped, but even I understand the risks, if those men are actually after me. But on the outside, there's people I can go to for help. People I know and trust.

"I can't stay here, Mikhail," I say softly. I don't know if it frightens me more to stay with him or leave, but at least on the outside, I'm free.

"But you have to all the same," he says to me with a tone of finality, stepping around me and going right for the door. "There's plenty of leftovers, and more food in the cupboards and fridge," he reminds me, but I don't care about those things.

"Wait!" I say, and try to follow after him, tugging at the door. But it's no use, he pulls it shut tight against my resistance, undaunted by my feeble attempts to stop him. And it slams shut. Leaving me alone inside.

"Damn it," I curse, and I find myself staring at the closed door, picturing him on the other side, filled with a sense of longing that definitely should not exist. I can still feel the imprint of his hand on my wrist, and I touch it tenderly before my heart drops and I return to my bland captivity without the spark of his presence.

CHAPTER 5
____

MIKHAIL

*S*he's a pain in the ass.

So why am I putting myself out on the line for her? *I don't kill women, I tell myself. No different than my sticking up for Nikita years ago.*

But that doesn't mean I have to go out of my way to save her. I could have just dumped her off somewhere with a warning, leave her fate in her own hands. But I know a girl like her has no way of understanding the trouble she's in, nor how serious it is. *Ditching her anywhere with a simple warning would have been the same as a death sentence. That's all.*

Why did I just sit and eat dinner with her? That's a question I can't answer as easily. I've never sat down and ate a meal with Nikita, not in all the years since I helped her upon arrival. When she was emaciated and starving after her trip over, I brought her food and left her to it.

I can't even remember the last time I actually sat and spoke with a woman casually over dinner. I may not hurt women, but I don't deal with them either.

Yet this one…
I have to get her out of my life quickly.

Chapter 6

Alicia

Things were so quiet in my little hideaway-slash-prison that I just cried myself to sleep after a news report about the murder of the congressman and the search for a missing witness. Me.

That's why it struck me as so odd, I guess, when I awake from my nap to the sound of movement. I'm put on edge immediately, because it could be anyone. Maybe it's my captor come back, or maybe it's the police. Or worst of all, it might be those mobsters out to eliminate the last witness.

That last possibility is the one that sticks out in my mind so much and makes my heart thump noisily in my chest, because it's the stuff my tortured dreams had been made of all night.

I get up, still dressed in the simple silk nightdress I'd found in the closet, my bare feet padding over the hard floor as I make my way out of the room.

I can hear the sounds, but they aren't coming from inside. It's like the sound of scuffing, mixed with the sound of metal. My heart is going haywire, and I creep closer to the door to hear. Light streams in from underneath, along that very narrow crack.

Grunting.

Oh lord, what if there's a fight happening outside my door right now?

I want to run and hide, but I know if they're here for me, hiding is only delaying the inevitable. If I'm going to live, I need to run.

But the door is locked...

I reach out with trembling fingers towards that cold metal door knob, and gently wrap my hand around it. I do my best to be quiet, but I'm no pro. I only hope the scuffle outside keeps them distracted as I turn...

And it opens. It's not locked.

I'm more surprised than thankful at first, but I very slowly open the door and peer out. The light blinds me for a second, but I squint through. Outside is a large brick hallway, and it seems to be empty but for the light spilling out of the room across the hall.

I creep out, my bare feet helping me stay quiet as I look to the elevator at the very end of the hallway. My heart leaps for joy!

But now, curiosity is getting the better of me, and I peer into the room across the hall. There, my captor awaits.

His back is mostly turned, but he's alone. All alone. The sounds I heard seem to be him working out. The room itself is just a bare-bones chamber, filled with gym equipment. Weights, pull-up bar, and more. But there he is, almost naked but for a pair of black boxer-briefs clinging to his thick thighs and groin.

I'm hypnotized watching him, frankly. He pulls himself

up as those glistening muscles bulge, biceps swelling so large as he seamlessly hoists up then eases himself back down, all control. He's well over six feet tall, and must weigh in excess of 200lbs of sheer muscle, but he moves with a certain grace that comes with that practiced workout.

He's engrossed in his routine, and now is the time to make my getaway…but here I am, staring at him instead. Gawking like a schoolgirl seeing a hunk working out for the first time. And in some ways, that feels so true. Because no guy I've seen before looks anything like this Mikhail.

He's tall, dark, and ruggedly handsome, sure. Ripped from head to toe, yeah. But those scars, those strange tattoos of his…all so unique. I can't deny the attraction and the curiosity I feel about him. Especially not since I'm standing here instead of running out into the street and finding my way home, like I should be doing.

I don't know if it's just the stress of the past few days, either, but watching him work out is getting me hornier than all hell. Not that cute kind of horny after a drink or two, or when you're with someone new. This is more primal than either of those things, and I catch the scent of his fresh sweat in the air, and that only helps to ignite the fire burning within me.

Everything he's told me has been the truth. He's been protecting me from someone far worse than him. But he's a killer. The conflicting thoughts swirl within me and then fade away to pure, simple, easy passion.

I can make a run for it.

Or I could walk into his gym, grab him through his boxer briefs, and work out my aggression on his body.

Part of my decision gets made for me, however, because with a grunt, he lets himself drop once more and speaks up.

"Are you going to stand there all day?" he asks in that deep, dark voice of his, so rich and delicious you could drizzle it over pancakes.

He hadn't needed to so much as turn to see me, and I can only presume my time spent staring gave me away somehow. But when his eyes turn towards me, so deep and smoldering, I feel a little weak in the knees.

Okay, a lot weak in the knees. Not even just the shock of him seeing me, but the way his body gleams with perspiration, and his gaze is locked on mine. Everything about him and his body calls out to me, and even though I should resist, I take a step forward.

And then another.

It's like I'm under his spell, though even I know it's only the spell of lust. Of frustration warped into desperate arousal.

Hearing the news report and knowing he was telling the truth, knowing that I'm really in danger, makes me want to feel alive. And this man, this killer, is the only one I know who can do that.

"You left my door unlocked."

He delays, and when finally says:

"Must have been an accident."

I know he's lying to me. It's easy to tell, because it's the first lie he's told. And while he might be the best killer on the planet for all that I've seen, he sucks at lying.

"You learn to spot a liar, working in a politician's office," I say, and he furrows his brow.

I'm in the presence of a military trained killer in better

physical condition than any man I've ever met. Standing right in front of his glistening, hard body, and I just called him a liar to his face.

"You really know how to try my patience," he says, but instead of turning away, he grabs me. Both hands. That strong grip of his taking hold of each hip as he pulls me right up against him. "What is it about you?" he growls in frustration, his voice so dark as his words rumble out, those eyes staring through me. Only the thin fabric separates us, and he's oh so close.

He feels amazing. Powerful and terrifying, all at once. The type of guy I should be running from, not the one that I should be subtly grinding against, but I can't help it. My hips work of their own accord, his hands gripping them but not impeding my motions. He could, if he wanted to.

I don't doubt that he could do nearly anything he wanted to to me. I've worked with a congressman, but Mikhail has real power. Not just physical power, but his personality, his control...

"What else do I do to you?"

Did I really just ask that?

His answer doesn't come like I expected though, it comes in the form of a throb. A heated pulse through his loins that swells out against me. His member rising beneath that thin layer of cotton over his groin, and rising fast.

He doesn't have any more words for me, because he reaches up with one hand, grasps the back of my hair, and tilts my head to the side.

He's in control now, there's no doubt of that, as there's no doubting the effect I'm having on his dick, and he lunges down, biting my neck, making me gasp, kissing at me with a desperate, carnal energy. To confirm, his other hand slips right around from my hip and grasps my rear, cupping the cheek and squeezing it tight.

My skin tingles with his kiss, my sex beginning to throb hard between my thighs. It's completely unlike me to be attracted to a guy like Mikhail, let alone feeling so hungry for his body. My fingers find his side, nails running over his hip until I meet his spine, and I pull him closer so that our bodies grind into one another with a heated urgency.

Then with such ease, he just pulls me up, lifting me with one hand as he kisses, licks, and bites at my tender neck. He's a powerhouse, and I get to feel those hardened pecs, abs, and biceps squeezing against me as he hefts me up. My groin positioned right atop his as that steely shaft pulses with life.

He finally breaks his hold on my neck to look into my eyes, his breathing heavy, not from the heavy workout, but from desire. And he growls his words at me.

"There is only one way this is going to end now, Alicia," he speaks my full name, his member pulsing as it rumbles off his tongue right before he pushes his lips against mine.

He tastes hot and spicy, like cinnamon mints, and my tongue eagerly presses against his. His words are like a warning, but they sound more like a promise to me, and my legs wrap around his hardened waist.

My heart thuds rapidly in my chest, and even though I'm being absolutely reckless, it only serves to turn me on more, and my arms wrap around his thick neck. His kiss is as brutal as he is, all control lost as he seeks to nearly bruise my lips against his, but it feels so right.

I can feel his hand pushing up under the silk nightie, and that hard hand grasps my bare flesh, squeezing my butt cheek so tightly. Each of those long fingers of his mesh with my own softer skin to make my nerves tingle, making the flesh bulge between.

"You play with fire," he growls in between smacks of our lips before I realize he's carried me over to the thick mat on the floor. Only the jarring sensation of his knees hitting the blue mattress-like material shakes me into realization of where we've moved.

I'm still held up in his arms, and he's fondling me, stroking those rough hands over my skin, along my rear, up alongside my breasts, touching their bare flesh beneath the silk. He's a real beast of a man, rough, hard, powerful.

Playing with fire seems to be putting it mildly.

But it's the only way I've ever felt so deliciously hot. None of the heavy petting with boyfriends past compared.

"I don't care," I whisper.

I watch his face as his hands trace over my skin with reverence and desire I've never experienced before. The intensity of the moment has us both under its spell, and I trace over his pecs. There's a wound near his collarbone and I can feel the remnants of stitches, and it intrigues me. I've never been with a man who had so many scars, so many marks left on him from a dangerous life.

I've also never been so turned on, and my fingertips wander lower, finding his hard abs and delving lower still.

Just as my dainty fingertips find the cotton bulge, he lowers my back onto the mat, laying me out before him as his smoldering eyes look down with such desire. Those powerful hands pull the night dress off me, almost tearing it in his drive to see me bare.

"I've never felt my cock get so hard over a lone woman before," he rumbles as my fingers touch that bulge again, graze it as I slip the tips along the waistband. And it's not hard to believe him, because that shaft is just so massive and thick. His rough, greedy hands go for my bare breasts, lavish them with such fond appreciation, and I can't help but cry out.

I stroke him, clumsily, the angle awkward and my spine arching to give him access to my chest. He palms by breasts, my nipples stiff against his flesh as I stare up at him wantonly.

"I've never needed someone so bad," I confess in return, my pussy screaming for attention as I rub his cock. My hips rise, but there's no pleasure to be found, not yet. He wants to experience me fully, despite my own ache, and I know the higher he builds me up, the more powerful the crash back to earth will be.

I tug upon the edge of his boxer-briefs, pulling them down, showing the V-shape of his cut abs leading on towards the tuft of dark hair and then…then…

My god…

The hefty shaft that spills out, rock-solid, is huge. Just immense! It's like the kind of thick, vein-ribbed shaft I'd have to doubt the reality of if I wasn't watching it pulse before my own eyes, standing out thick and full of heated blood.

And while I stare agape, he slides his hands down from my chest, curls his digits into the waistband of my panties, and pulls them off. He wads them up into a ball and takes a brief inhale of my scent upon them before he pushes his thumbs into my soft inner thigh flesh, spreading me open wide and staring at my slit.

"I'm going to fucking stretch you so wide, silly girl," he rumbles, leaning over me as his boxer-briefs slip further down, and those two heavy balls spill out beneath his shaft.

It's a threat and a promise wrapped into one delicious sentence, and I reward him with a nip of his lower lip between my teeth. I'm inciting the beast within him, testing his patience and resolve, but I don't care. I want to see how far I can push him, and how far he'll push me back.

His cock pulses in my palm, the veins prodding my flesh as I squeeze him, tempting him closer to my slickened mound.

His chest swells as he looms over me, and he pulls me close by his grasp on my legs, so that the thick tip of his manhood grazes my slit, smearing some of my honey upon his covered shaft. He leans in over me, like I'm prey caught by this magnificent predator, and he bites my lip in return as his cock throbs against me.

"My name will be written on your lips by the time you're done screaming," he pledges, just before he angles back his hips, then jabs his cock at me! That thick member pierces me with one hard thrust, stretching me out so incredibly wide it makes my eyes widen, my spine arch, and my throat sing.

It's the best parts of heaven and hell combined, and for a moment, my world just stops. Everything outside this room, all my worries and fears, they disappear, and all I can think of is him. His gorgeous body has silenced the demons in my head.

My nails dig into his back, legs locked around his ass.

Only something really fucking wrong can feel this good, and fucking a near stranger raw was definitely wrong.

The man who killed my boss, held me captive…has me pinned to the mat, speared upon his dick. And he's looking down at me with such lust in his eyes, knowing it's only begun.

My nails claw at him, but it's like trying to tear into steel, and he begins to rock his hips, pistoning that thick cock at a slow rate to start. My poor little cunt, ripped asunder and now stretched raw around his shaft as he begins to take me. His low, rumbling moans sounding so vicious and bestial.

It's just what I need.

Just what I want.

"Oh god," I whimper, and for a second, I don't know if I can take anymore. My body begins to quiver, and I'm filled with a sudden sensation I wasn't expecting until much later. He's only just barely hilted within me, but his cock was made for me with how quickly my nerves respond.

The beginnings of an orgasm start to unfurl within me, and I gasp.

Watching that glistening, muscled torso rippling over me through narrow slits, I moan and writhe, my body tensing as that pleasure builds. Mikhail's like no other man I've known, and the situation is completely out there.

It's so many layers of wrong and right done just so. My toes curl, and he's only begun to pound into me. Again and again, that thick cock pummels my poor, pink pussy, his heavy, cum-laden balls battering against my pale rear as he hammers down.

And while his chest still gleams with perspiration, I can

get a glimpse of his godlike cock glistening with a different kind of slickness: my own, and I'm so wet it's embarrassing.

I've never felt like this before, and definitely never done something so risky, but it all pays off almost too quickly as my nerves tighten and then release, pleasure flooding me. I can't believe it, but I'm trembling against him like a virgin, my screams echoing off the Spartan walls. My thighs tighten around his waist, but he's too powerful to stay put.

Instead, he grinds into me, as deeply as he can, and it's too much and yet perfect all at once, that pain and pleasure culminating into the most powerful orgasm I've ever imagined having.

Mikhail pummels me throughout my loud climax, pumping harder even as a gush of warm honey coats his shaft and covers his balls. That hefty sac of his slapping against me wetly now as he keeps me pinned beneath him, manipulating my legs as his cock throbs, swelling out and stretching me as he moans.

"Mmph," he groans, "your tight little cunt was made for wrapping around my cock, you screaming beauty."

I feel like I'm on drugs, the rush of his body taking me to new heights. His words tease me higher, and I'm squirming like a girl as each pulse, each thrust, sends a delightful aftershock through me.

Sex has never been like this before. I never dreamed it could be.

"Oh *god*, Mikhail," I gasp, my throat raw from all my screaming, my mind emptied of everything but him. "You're amazing!"

His steely body is like a freight train, and just works

with such fierce precision. He pounds me through my climax, blasts the fog from my head as I squeal and moan atop his manhood. One of those thick, bulging biceps pushes into the base of my spine as he lifts me, still jackhammering into my raw pussy.

"From the moment I saw you, I knew I had to protect you…fuck you…breed you," he growls into my ear before biting into my neck. "If you stay, that's what'll happen to you, *kotika*."

It's crass and dirty, and I'm hungry for more.

My head tilts to the side, giving him access to my slender neck, the skin there so delicate as he marks me as his own. Hours ago, all I could think about was getting away, but now I know I really want to run from my feelings. From my dangerous attraction to this killer.

I can feel my own body overheating, so hot as the perspiration builds between us and my breasts bounce, gleaming in the light as we rut. His Russian curses tickle my ears as he swells within me, and the mat strains beneath us.

He pushes me back down into the mat, pinning me down beneath his powerful arms and battering me with that thick trunk of a dick.

"You're not done yet," he promises with a gravelly husk, "you're going to come on my cock one more time before I finish in you." And it's a promise he plans to deliver on as he reaches a thumb towards my clit, ready to torture that poor bud.

I'm already so overwhelmed with sensations, but he makes me feel so dirty. I want more, like a hedonist, and my hand grasps his, pushing him down harder. But then, before I can even get close, his free hand grabs my wrist, pinning it to the mat above me, all without skipping a beat.

His weight presses down upon me and our bodies writhe in unison as my slickness lets his fingers glide over my throbbing clit. We're making a mess on the mat, my juices running down between my thighs and over his heavy sac.

But he doesn't care, he's enraptured with me, forcing his eyes open to soak me in as he tweaks my clit, circles it, prods me to new heights beneath him. He's pounding so hard and fast it's blinding, and I watch as his broad jaw clenches and his dick swells, stretching me wider, making it twinge and hurt a little.

"Come for me, little kitten, or you'll be so sore you'll not walk for weeks," he growls in threat.

And his words... Those dark, dangerous words spoken in that delicious accent...

That's the final nail in my coffin. My pussy tightens around him, milking him, knowing full well the risk I'm taking and how stupid I'm being, but needing it all the same. Good girls don't get knocked up by killers. Good girls don't take risks with dark and mysterious men they don't know.

So maybe I am a little bit bad, deep down, and he's just teasing it out of me. Along with a whole bunch of explosive pleasure.

His neck tenses as he watches me, and as I scream out again, he pummels me with his cock, swelling inside me as he barrels his way towards his own finale. This ruthless, cold-hearted killer, all muscle, sinew, and murderous-intent, holding me as he hammers into my pussy.

"You're going to take it," he growls, and that thick,

battering ram of a cock explodes inside me, shooting thick gouts of creamy seed. A deep, dark, velvety moan of pleasure escapes his lips as he shudders, emptying his loins into me.

And then his mouth crashes against mine, burning hot, lust tracing from his tongue to mine. He's not gentle, his every motion speaking of just how powerful his emotions for me are. Not even the calm and in-control Mikhail can hold them back, and that sends another illicit thrill up my spine. He's opened the Pandora's Box inside of me.

There's no turning back now, I tell myself.

But fate has a way of throwing you.

CHAPTER 7

MIKHAIL

I lift her body up into my arms, because somehow, it just doesn't seem right to let her to wake up on a gym mat. Her sleep schedule is still wonky, but she was clearly exhausted after the ordeal she's been through.

She's a damn frustrating woman. I left her door unlocked so she could leave, and I could be free of her. But she stuck around instead. Broke down my last barrier. And that is dangerous for us both.

Carrying her into the bedroom, I lay her beautiful figure out with care. She sends a pang through my heart when I think of how I was about to let her wander off, get herself killed, just so that these feelings might finally subside. Shame fills me as my heart beats quicker.

A coward's way out.

That's what I tried to take. To wash my hands of responsibility. But her blood would've been on my hands regardless, and it'd never wash clean. I know that.

Looking down at her, those long, beautiful tresses

framing her face, her body beautifully angelic in the nude, I know I have to make the hard choices. For her sake.

She can't stay. I can't play the role of lover.

CHAPTER 8

ALICIA

I wake up to the drab grey sight of my prison's ceiling, though it doesn't bother me so much anymore. As much as I feel embarrassed for making a pass at the man who abducted me—and then giving into passion and sleeping with him—I just want to feel his comforting touch.

Rolling over, I reach out, but he's not there.

I look around and see that the room is empty. Only me. And I feel a loneliness deep down that hurts my heart.

Abandonment.

I crave his warmth wrapping around me, taking me again with such reckless abandon. It's so unlike me to give in so readily, so eager to just have him take me. Maybe it's the isolation of this place, I try to convince myself, but I know that isn't it.

There's something deeper within me that pulls me to him. For the first time, I actually have feelings for someone. More than lust or a high school crush, something deeper and darker than I could possibly bring myself to understand. I want my life to be tied to his, always.

But now he's gone, and I don't know what that means. Back in my cell, left to wonder about how he feels. Does he regret it? Is that why he brought me back here and left?

I push myself out of bed, my thoughts quickly growing morbid. Of course he regrets it. To him, I'm just some floozy who got in over her head, a distraction. He thinks of me as his troublesome obligation, so of course he'd extract some payment.

Plodding my way morosely to the bathroom, I expect to see bags under my eyes, but aside from the hurt lingering in my green eyes, I actually look healthy and rested. Maybe I did just need to get laid. Maybe I used him, just like he used me.

But even as I try to convince myself, I know it's a lie.

By the time I finish tidying up, I hear the sounds of my large protector returning. His footsteps thud in the hallway outside before the door swings open and he looks in on me. That rugged, handsome face of his is completely serious.

There's no trace of the passion that was there the night before, and I feel my heart constrict in my chest.

"You didn't spend the night."

"I had to arrange a few things," he says, stepping inside and handing me a brown paper bag with a travelling cup full of coffee, I presume. "We're taking a trip."

I notice that he's dressed in a nice maroon shirt, unbuttoned at the collar where some of his dark hair pokes out, and a black jacket over top.

He almost looks ready for a date in those dark denim jeans.

And my life suddenly explodes with color, and I smile instantly. It's like all my fear and apprehension have been completely melted away within a second flat.

"Really? We're leaving? Ohh, are we going somewhere warm to hide out for a few months until the heat dies down?"

"I'm going to drive you out of state, to a place I know well, to be safe with some people I trust," he says with that hard stoicism of his. "As soon as you're ready, I'll take you out to the car and we'll be done. You can eat breakfast as I drive," he explains, laying down the sack and coffee upon the table.

"Sure, well...not like I have much here to pack," I say with a roll of my eyes, heading to grab the few things I have scattered about. "And I'm assuming we're probably not going to stop off at my place to get my luggage." I'm trying to keep things light, but the fact that I can't read him at all, that I don't know what he's thinking, is throwing me off.

Especially since he looks so damn good today.

"I'll give you money to buy whatever you want where we're going," he says, reaching into his jacket and pulling out a wallet. He flips it open and slides out a credit card, offering it to me. "There's no limit, just try not to make a huge scene once we're there," he explains.

"So don't go *Pretty Woman* on you. Got it," I say with a sly wink. Tugging on the casual yoga jacket he'd brought me earlier, and slipping into my dangerously high heels, I look like a pampered housewife leaving rehab.

But there's definitely pep to my step, and I grab my coffee, heading towards the door.

"Road trip time!"

He leads the way on down out of the building, locking up behind him. We come out onto the street, where a beautiful black sedan awaits us, shiny and new, looking like it just rolled off an assembly line. Mikhail pushes a pair of sunglasses down over his eyes as he keeps watching, but makes it to the passenger side door before me to hold it open.

"Be natural, calm," he assures me as I stand at the edge of freedom once more. Though not quite.

But it's a step up. And the fresh air is wonderful, so I slip into his car and relax back into the plush seat. It's roomy and reminds me of traveling in the back of the limo with Mr. Gallego. I have to push that thought aside, though. I'm still not ready to grapple with that.

When he slides into the driver side, I give him what I hope to be my most radiant smile. "Haven't you noticed? I'm always calm."

Mikhail gives me a bemused, uneven smile as he starts up the car and we begin to pull out.

"It's not a joyride—you need to get away from here. Away from all of this, where it's safe," he explains as the city passes me by. "I have people very close to me out of state who can keep you secure, away from prying eyes, as this all blows over. These are good people. Solid like the earth."

"I get it. I mean, I don't. This is way over my head, and you aren't exactly a giving conversationalist, but... I trust you. I know it must be really serious," I say. I know it's important to him that I understand he's not trying to be a jerk keeping me locked up. At least, I think so.

My words seem to reassure him, because my Russian giant of a man quiets up and keeps his eyes ahead. He takes us through the concrete jungle of New York with great care, no cop in the world having reason to stop us.

As we come to the bridge leading out of the city, a toll booth looms, and we wait in line.

"So how do you know these people?" I ask, just trying to drum up conversation.

"The leader of this club is my brother," he says in his gravelly, low voice. "He has full run of the area. All his people are loyal, committed. They are to be trusted."

Though thoughts of being hidden among a... *club* are more than a little upsetting to me. I know what he really means.

"So we'll be staying with a *gang*, is what you're saying?" I ask with a little more panic in my voice than I intended.

He shushes me silently as it comes our turn to pay the toll.

"We'll be staying with friends and family," he informs me as the toll booth operator watches with particular interest to us both. Maybe it's the car. It does stand out, even in this crowd. "And don't call it that when you're with them. They're sensitive to that, *da*?"

I keep quiet until the window is back up and we're on the move again.

"Right, but how is a *gang* going to be safe for me, Mikhail?" I ask, earnest in my fear. Everything about my life, ever since the party, has been terrifying. And the only constant has been Mikhail. Quiet, imposing, in control...

I should trust him more, especially after last night, and so my hand reaches out to rest on top of his. I can feel the thick, bulging veins upon the back of his powerful hand jutting out so prominently. They remind me of another part of him, a more private part, that pulsed with blood and veins.

"I know you wouldn't take me somewhere unsafe," I finally say, taking a deep breath.

His gaze flicks down towards our hands, then over at me.

"A *gang* as you call it—a family—is the only thing that will keep you safe, my *kotika*," he says. "These are good people. Not like me. They do what they do because they must. They do not deal like mobsters," he explains to me patiently.

"I have a feeling that if you weren't a good person, I'd be dead by now," I murmur, not ready to admit that fully. It sends a cold shiver up and down my spine just saying the words, a pit of heavy dread in my stomach. My hand tightens upon his, and I relax.

"You presume upon my character too much," he says, but he leaves it at that as we settle into the rest of the drive. My mind is left to wonder at all the ways in which he thinks himself not a good man. And of what that means for our future.

I'm so distracted I barely notice the maroon car that's still behind us. I recall glimpsing one just like it since the moment we left the toll bridge.

CHAPTER 9

MIKHAIL

The old neighborhood.

The dingy docks, no longer as bustling as they once were, lining the shorefront. The buildings mostly old and peculiar. But there's a simple sort of humble homecoming feeling to it. Even if I never called Bayonne home, it was a home that always awaited me, if I wanted it.

"Are we nearly there?" Alicia asks, and I nod.

"Yes, this is the area. The club will look out for you," I say, knowing it to be true. Part of me wishes I had long ago taken the invitation to join this crew. But a bigger part of me knows it was never my destiny. I had too much of a man's ego back then, and now? Now I'm too bloodied.

There's no getting out of the Bratva, not now. I know too much. I'm too valuable to them, and they might have me killed if they ever found out I was even toying with the idea of leaving. Hell, Gregorovich would have me killed for a lot less than that if he thought he could get away with it. He just needs an excuse, and my leaving a witness alive?

That's one hell of an excuse.

"Smells like burning rubber or something," Alicia says, turning up her nose, but I can see her looking around with renewed interest. Her hand hasn't left mine the entire drive, and her touch is driving me fucking crazy, but I can't show her how much she's getting in under my skin. I'm afraid I showed her too much already, letting down my guard with her last night.

"Some might find it a dingy place, but it's old and fiercely independent," I say to her, realizing my fondness for the place goes a little deeper than I realize. I take us down a road, heading towards *The Glass*, a club where I'm to meet Leon.

She looks at me, and I get the feeling she can see right through me to the core, to the truths I hide away from everyone.

"How is it you know this place so well?" she asks, perceptive as I feared.

I lick my lips, hesitating a moment. I'm not a very personable guy. You share too much with people, it gets used against you. I've seen it a thousand times, over and over again. If it's not a fellow gunman in the bratva, it's a man's wife ratting him out, or his best friend. His brother.

But I can't help myself with her.

"It was where I first arrived in America. Hidden in one of those shipping containers back there," I say, hooking a thumb over my shoulder. "The *bratva* arranged it all with the Union Club, and from there…I went on to New York to really sink my teeth into business."

"Oh," she says, accepting it all as if that were the normal way to come to America. Her brows furrow in thought, and I can't help but wonder what's racing through her mind. She'd been clever, locked in her little cell. I had to keep a close eye on her the entire time, making sure she stayed put, but someone like her can't be locked up forever. A keen mind and a youthful exuberance for life...

At least here she'd have some entertainment, some other people to talk to who can keep her out of trouble. It's for the best.

"How long ago was that?"

"Very long ago," I say, not wanting to go into any more detail than that. I am a few years her senior after all, and I don't care much for reflecting on the passage of time my own self.

It's a nice little town, all in all, and I decide to change the subject with some info on the place. "This is a quiet place, the club keeps things like that. Keeps the violence and drugs out."

I see it up ahead, the club we're headed towards. The Glass sounds fancier than it really is, and that much becomes apparent by the rows of motorcycles lined up outside.

"Yea, I read about it in the news, a biker gang that helps 12 year old girls stand up to their abusive parents. I guess they can add helping out damsels in distress to their list too," she says, her saucy mouth curling into a wicked smile that makes me instantly want to crush her lips against mine.

Her emerald eyes twinkle as she looks at me, and I think she's even daring me to.

And just about as my resolve is about to crumple, a knock at the window cockblocks me.

It's Leon.

I push open the door immediately and stand up to the guy. He's a big man himself now, but I do my best to loom as ominously over him as I can.

"*The Lone Wolf*," he says darkly to me. "You've got some fucking nerve coming back into this town."

CHAPTER 10

ALICIA

The entire drive, Mikhail seemed different. But for those few seconds, I really thought he'd return some affection, or at least acknowledge it. It's not that he's been distant, not really, because he chatted more casually the entire trip. It took longer than expected, since when we first arrived Mikhail took one look at the bar and somehow instantly knew the guy he wanted wasn't there. He plays coy, but I'm guessing it's just because the guy's motorcycle wasn't out front. We drove around, and he treated me to a meal before we returned at night.

I just don't know where we stand, and it's super awkward to not know if it was a one-night stand, and if I'm just blowing things out of proportion. For all my partying, I've never done what I did with Mikhail last night, and I can still smell his skin on mine.

But now he's standing toe-to-toe with some guy who looks built like a brick wall, same as him. I feel like I'm going to finally see what happens when an unstoppable force meets an immovable object, and I shrink back in my seat.

The two men have an ominous stare-off, both huge and looking ready for a fight. This new guy is wearing leather, and has the appearance of a more traditional thug though, some motorcycle gangers. I have no idea what to expect, so I just hold my breath and hope for the best as I get out of the car. Mikhail wouldn't take me to someplace we were *both* in danger, would he? Maybe he assumed the wrong things about these people...

This new guy cracks his knuckles, drawing my eye to the many rings on his fingers. Mikhail moves a hand towards his hip where a gun is hid, and then, in a flash everything is going down! The new thug moves his elbow up to smack Mikhail in the nose, and Mikhail jabs right for the kidneys.

I shriek!

Both guys are frozen though, stopping just short of impact on one another before they wrap their arms about the other and embrace. Meanwhile, my heart is racing like mad. *Great first impression, Allie.*

"Leon! You're quicker than ever," Mikhail says with a smile.

"Quick enough to put a fright into your Old Woman," Leon says, shooting a half-smirk over towards me before breaking the embrace with Mikhail. "My most sincere apologies, ma'am," he says, sounding rather contrite for a gangster.

"I was just the audience," I spit back, embarrassed by my own fear. This whole situation has me more on edge than I want to admit.

"Sorry, my timid *kotika*," Mikhail says, releasing the

other guy and stepping around the car to extend his hand to me. "Come, meet Leon—he is a brother to me. Leon, this is Alicia," he says, putting his arm around me, holding me close.

"Ahh, she is indeed a pussycat," Leon says, taking my hand, and despite his gruff appearance, lifting it up and kissing my knuckles like a prince. "Welcome to Bayonne, Alicia," he says so dashingly.

I'd probably have a schoolgirl crush on him if it weren't for the fact that Mikhail is finally showing some affection back. All I can think about is the sensation of his arm draped around me, and I can feel the flush rising to my cheeks.

"Thanks," I say to Leon before smiling up at Mikhail. "I'm excited to meet some friends of Mikhail, let alone a brother."

"Now hands off of her," Mikhail says in a lower voice, pushing away Leon's arm, though the two clearly are being playful with one another. My guardian leads me inside as the other bikers clamor around while we head on into the club. A few of them grin and cheer excitely for Mikhail's return, others look on as if watching a very important person arrive for a political stop.

The energy in the room is strange. It's similar to when I was working for Mr. Gallego in some ways, but with him, I never felt people were truly happy to see him. It was more like they needed to see him but wished they didn't have to.

With Mikhail, these people want him to be here, even if they are being respectful. He's being treated like an important person, and I have to admit... I like it. It makes me feel proud to be on his arm.

"Some people you know?" A pretty but somewhat unkempt woman asks, stepping close to Leon's side, draping an arm over his shoulder. But hey, I've not had a chance for a good sprucing up in a while either, so who am I to talk?

"Yeah," Leon chuckles, "it's been a hell of a long time, but I like to think I know him. He's the walking, talking reminder of my past, in more ways than one, but dammit, he's family. You two, meet my gal, Cherry."

She looks like a Cherry, all fiery red mane and soft features.

"You mean…" Cherry murmurs.

"Yeah," Leon replies, stepping forward to give Mikhail a tight hug. "This towering giant is my brother, both by blood and by the Bratva," he says, looking back at Cherry with a rugged smile.

"She's a beauty, I can see why you want to keep her safe, brother. We both have excellent taste," Leon says, slapping Mikhail's shoulder and smiling pleasantly over at me.

"You should see me when I haven't been locked up for an eternity without a lick of makeup or a decent shampoo," I say with a grin, though I feel far more flattered than I'm letting on. Leon's definitely a ladies' man.

But the warmth coming from Mikhail is what's really driving me wild.

We head to the bar, with Mikhail stopping to give passing greetings now and then until drinks are brought over and poured.

"Uh, let's go in the back and discuss this, eh?" Leon says with his arm around Cherry's waist. He has little hint of an accent, just a harsh voice and way of talking.

"I need you to help me hide Alicia, *bratishka*," Mikhail says as we enter the enclosed back room, just the four of us. "A few months should do the trick. Then I'll come back and see she's sent along safely," he says, and my heart stops.

"You'll come back?" I ask without thinking, my head turned towards him and my brow raised. I can feel the anger start to boil within me, and even the weight of his arm wrapped around me can't stop this sick feeling from rolling around in my stomach.

But he ignores me.

"Mikhail, I don't know if we can do that right now," Leon says sadly, shaking his head. I can tell it pains him greatly to disappoint his brother. "The FBI is on our backs, brother, and there's not a single place in this town we could hide her without them sniffing her out. It just isn't safe here in Bayonne. It's not like it used to be when we were boys."

"*Pozhaluysta.* I beg of you," Mikhail answers, a pleading edge to his tone.

"What happened to the usual safe houses?" Leon asks, frowning.

Mikhail looks aside as though embarrassed. "They've been…compromised."

"What? How did that—" Leon bites his tongue, and I wonder if he doesn't want to know. If what Mikhail does, if who he is, is so unpalatable, then it's just better not knowing. I'm on the brink of tears, but I hold it back. I'm not going to be a blubbering mess.

"I need to get her somewhere. She won't last in the city."

"You're going to leave me for a few months? Just like

that?" I ask, and even though I'm holding back tears, I don't bother trying to contain the hurt in my voice. The anxiety I've felt since this morning is just rising up within me, and I can't hold it back it anymore.

"It's what has to be done. If I'm missing from the city for a long time, then it'll raise suspicions, which endangers you further," Mikhail says to me in his deep, husky voice. He's frustrated with me, I can tell. His brow furrows, and he looks about to say something harsh. All the same, his hand and arm squeezes tighter.

"I am no good for you, *kotika*," he says to me in a low, gravelly voice. "You slept with a killer. That was a huge mistake. Do you really want to compound it by sticking around him and risking it becoming more?" he pushes, those dark eyes of his wide, taunting me with the truth. "You are a good girl. And when this all blows over, you can go back to living a good girl's life. Not hanging out with thugs in a bar, hanging off the arm of a contract killer."

He steals the words from my mouth, the thoughts from my mind. Part of me knows he's right. That he's giving me a chance to move on, to find something else in my life.

But everything I know has been tossed upside-down. I have no job, and I can't talk to any of my old colleagues, and I'm supposed to sit here for a few months with these people I don't know...

And the thing that's bothering me the most is that I don't want him to leave. What does that say about me, after what he just said? Why didn't that repulse me like it should? It does, partly, but it also fills me with a lustful heat that I don't want to acknowledge. But my hand moves to his jaw, and I stroke it tenderly, because I don't know what to say but I don't want him to go.

"I need your help, too. I think… maybe we can work out a deal," Leon says, intruding on our private moment.

"I will help you in any way I can. Whatever you need," Mikhail says, and his tone sends a chill down my spine. He sounds so serious. So dire.

"I need you to eliminate someone for me."

"Leon, what's going on? What do you mean, 'eliminate' someone?" Cherry's voice sounds far away, shrill and distant, and then all sound is lost to me. I move to a chair, placing myself down carefully. I can't hear, I can't think. It's all too much to bear.

All that I can see and think of is a flash of a memory that I couldn't remember, the man looking at me in the room of red, a gun pointed in my direction. Mikhail. Right before he decided to spare me.

Is this what having a breakdown feels like? I never thought a person could be aware of so much and nothing all at once. It's like my life has come to razor focus, and it has to cut out all the noise for me to process what this all means. Who Mikhail really is.

He's the guy that people hire to kill. He's everything he warned me he is.

The sound of my name pulls me from my spell, and I look up at the three of them. I have no idea how much time has passed, but based on how concerned Mikhail looks, I must be pale as a sheet.

"I promise to find a safe place to hide Alicia in the meantime. I have friends and connections all over town. Don't worry, *moy brat*."

"*Spasibo*, Leon," Mikhail says, but his eyes don't leave mine.

I'm a fool who's fallen for a bad man, just like that. And I've fallen hard. I don't know how to pull myself from this. Blonde hair tickles my burning cheeks, and my heart thumps heavily in my chest. I should let him go, forget what we did last night, the passion I feel for him. Just walk away from it all.

"Don't worry about Alicia," Leon tells Mikhail as if I'm not right here. I feel like a child being led around by my teachers, unable to speak up for myself or even put a voice to the jumbled thoughts rumbling through my mind. "I know a club up in Jersey City that owes me a favor and has a safe house where I've personally lain low a few times. She'll be safe and comfortable. My vice-prez will take her there. Eva? Got anything going on tomorrow?"

"Nah, I can tell my techs to handle things 'till the afternoon."

"Good. Do that—I've gotta call in a favor from someone I know I can trust. My brother here has a lady he needs taken to the safe house the boys up in Jersey City run. Some of them will still be awake at this hour. If not, here's some cash for a motel overnight. Get her in there first thing in the morning. Tell them things are even between us if they get this taken care of, alright?"

"Been a long time since I've been uptown... So am I following you, big guy?" Eva says to Mikhail.

"I appreciate it," Mikhail says to Eva before turning to his brother. "Leon, you should know of all people that I act swiftly and quietly. Once I'm off to handle this situation, it won't be long before it is done."

"I know. Tomorrow night, I'm guessing?"

Mikhail nods.

"Alright. I can work with that. It's been good to see you again, Mikhail."

"*Da svidaniya, Leon.*"

"*Fsyevo harosheva, moy brat.*"

The night air gives me a hint of life again, but as Mikhail helps me into the car, I don't feel at all like myself. Since he's held me captive, I've felt a gamut of emotions for him. Hatred, anger, annoyance...but underpinning it all has been something that I haven't been ready to grapple with.

I'm alive because of him. Because he couldn't bring himself to kill me. Because he wanted me to live, even if it meant taking away my life and my freedom. And some part of me knows that it wasn't an easy decision for him.

Did he feel something for me from the very start?

I glance over at him as he drives, his expression serious and lost in thought. The lights cast deep shadows along him, but it only makes him look more rugged.

I relax in my seat, exhausted from the long day and too worn-down to even fret about the fact that he wants to abandon me. I know he thinks it's for my own safety, but now, I can't help but want to be near him. In a weird way, I feel safer with him nearby.

What a laugh that is. He's my captor, right? I should be wanting him to leave me so I can make an escape and check in on my mom, but instead, I feel connected to him in a way I've never felt before.

The drive feels short, but I know it's only because I keep dozing off. When we pull up to the place we're staying, though, I look over at him.

"Will you at least stay with me a night?" I finally ask,

my voice sounding so faint as I reach over and touch his muscular arm.

He stares over at me in the dim light of the streetlamp, determination written upon his gorgeously rugged face. Determination that is quickly becoming wavering resolve.

CHAPTER 11

MIKHAIL

We pull up to the motel and Eva explains a few things to me.

"Keep inside as much as you can—we've got a crew nearby, but best she's not seen. Head off any trouble, right?" she says after pointing out a few things. I take the keys to the room.

"Thank you, I'll make sure she understands the importance of it," I say before turning back to the starry-eyed woman, so in over her head. I put a hand upon her back and guide her upstairs into the building. It's a motel, but it's clean. And most importantly, it comes with a back exit, in case they come for her.

I want to be gone, but she's clinging to me like she never wants me to leave her sight. It's quite a shift from when she first woke up in my safehouse and tried so desperately to build up walls around herself. I don't know if I should be happy or terrified by the change.

I should just leave and break her heart. Make the

motion quick, like removing a Band-Aid, but the second I said I'd stay, it was like her soul lit up the car. I've never had that kind of effect on people. I've never let myself get close enough to anyone...

"Better than my place," she says as we close the door behind us. I lock it, then start to look around the room. I have to be able to navigate the room in the dark, just in case.

Alicia, meanwhile, heads right to the bed and takes off her ridiculously high heels.

"I don't know how trophy wives do this. Six inch stilettos are for dinner and dancing only, not sitting in a car for*ever*," she says, but her voice is light and airy.

I can't help myself, my gaze taken from the task of surveilling the room to look her over again. Her beautiful body is hidden beneath the pink yoga outfit I bought her but doing little to keep me from the memory of how she really looks beneath it all.

"There are worse things such women have to do," I mutter, knowing where this is going. And knowing even more intimately what it is I have to do. For her own damn good.

"Yea, I'm sure spending sprees on someone else's credit card is *exhausting*," she teases with a flip of her long, blonde hair. She seemed so tired in the car, but now she's perked up, her sense of humor returning. I force myself not to grin, though, and she cocks her head at me, her beautiful green eyes twinkling with mischief.

She thinks she knows what she's doing, but she doesn't. Sitting there like a vixen, leaning back just enough to show off the outline of her breasts beneath the stretchy fabric, her legs crossed so that I can see the curve of her ass, she feels like a temptress.

But I'm a man she doesn't want to tempt.

I stride over toward her, reach out a hand. My calloused, ringed fingers sliding along her smooth, ivory cheek and back into her blonde hair. She tempts me, but she shouldn't. I need to show her that.

"The kept woman of a mobster like me doesn't just get to spend and relax," I growl at her, my voice deep and menacing. I should know, I've seen many a man wet himself to my threats. "She has to earn it. Not just on her back, *kotika*," I lick my lips, because as much as I'm being threatening, the thoughts are exciting me, "but on her knees."

I watch her thoughts as they pass over her expression. Her curiosity melds into fear and desire all at once. It's an intriguing mix, and her emerald eyes watch as I lick my lips and say the crass words. As a hitman, I have to be perceptive of everything, to every last twitch of a human face.

Usually it's because I need to know when and how to kill someone.

This time it's helpful, because I can see how excited she's becoming, just by the flush in her cheeks and the way her chest rises and falls more quickly with her light breaths.

"Is that what you want?"

"That's how it is," I say, not exactly a direct answer, but it'll do. I let my long fingers toy with her hair, my thumb brush her cheek and trace along her pretty face. "You didn't think going down this road with me would be all sunshine and fairy tales, did you?" I ask, arching a brow and stepping in closer, my height advantage making me tower over her shapely form so menacingly. "Men like me demand a lot of their women."

I've never been like this with women. In fact, I loathe the way the other mobsters push their girls around, cheat on them, use them. It's the actions of tiny, insecure men.

But this isn't for my benefit. It's for hers.

She's still trying to be brave, but I can feel the little tremor that tenses at her temple. I can see the way she looks towards the door, just for the briefest of moments before a smile touches her lips.

"I already survived round one, Mikhail."

She's still brazen, and I know I have to break that from her if I'm to knock any sense into her. So I move my hand around to the back of her head, knitting my fingers through her blond hair as I take hold. Then the pressure starts as I push her downwards, my free hand going to my waist, undoing the zipper on my pants.

"Then show me," I husk. "Show me you've got what it takes to be a killer's woman."

Her body tenses for a second at the added pressure as she drops lower, but then she's reaching out, one hand on my thigh, the other going for my cock as I let the thick, growing shaft loose of my pants. Her breathing gets harder, but she licks her full lips, and then she's licking the tip of my crown, her eyes fluttering up to look at me as she does so.

It'd be the prettiest sight in the world, if it weren't for what it means.

Her mouth wraps around the head of my dick, slowly teasing her way down, trying to set her own pace.

I'm rock-solid in no time, and my cock is swelling to fullness in her mouth, stretching those pretty lips of hers. It's such a lewd display, and my dick throbs with excitement as she begins to work me into her warm, wet mouth. I love the feel, and my veiny shaft never looked so good as it does crammed into her pretty face like this.

I can't resist but give a moan.

"That's a good girl," I say without realizing it, enjoying this more than I intended as I stroke her hair and push her head in, making her move a little faster. Make her take me a little deeper.

She braces herself against my thigh but doesn't resist. She has something to prove now, I realize too late, and I'm not positive which one of us will come out the winner.

Her tongue trails along my veins, her dark lashes fluttering down to hide her gaze from me as she lets out a low moan of appreciation. She shifts on the bed, positioning herself so she can take me deeper, my heavy hand urging her on.

My cock glistens with her saliva as her mouth pulls back, those pouty lips dragging along the thick veins until she's suckling upon the very tip. And I'm finding myself more taken with this than I should. I was meaning to show her the truth of things, instead I was making myself crave her deeper.

I give her head a bit more of an aggressive push until my balls are smacking her chin with the motions of her mouth, and I growl out.

"A mobster's girl has to take it. Any time, any place… any which way he needs it," I tell her, sounding so possessive. Letting my brutishness out more. Untying the restrained beast within.

But that's dangerous, even for teaching a lesson. Because deep down, there's so much I want to do to this woman…change her forever. Make her mine. Mark her permanently.

Chapter 12

Alicia

I'm nearly choking on his huge cock, but I can't give up. I feel like he wants me to prove myself, to show him that he's not going to break me. That I can handle him, at his best and worst.

I don't know why I need to prove this so badly, not just to himself, but to me. I've never had these feelings for anyone before. Not like this.

When he said he was going to leave, I swear I felt my heart break. And if I can make him stay with a blowjob? It's going to be the best goddamned blowjob anyone has ever received in their life.

He has me pinned against him, though, and I'm barely able to move but for the wiggle of my tongue, spreading the thick saliva over more of his cock. Tentatively I reach down, finding the sac beneath, grasping it lightly in my hands. It's a contrast from the aggressive face fucking, the tender rolling of his balls between my digits, but with how he's moaning, I know I'm winning him over.

He sheds his jacket, and then there's just the shirt beneath, hugging his muscles as I make his chest heave with his rising breaths. He's so big in my mouth that it hurts my jaw to stretch this wide, but I'm committed. Partly it's because I tell myself I want him on my side, to protect me, but really I know that's a convenient lie. I'm drawn to him on a base level. It's that and that alone that makes me lash my tongue along the thick, bulging veins of his dick with such attention, cradle his balls with such affection.

Then finally, he unbuttons his shirt, and I see the rippling muscles beneath. Those thick pecs and abs unveiled as he sheds his clothes.

"Just the beginning," he says with a husky roar, grasping my shoulders and prying me off his cock so that the long, thick member throbs in the open air, glistening with my saliva as he pushes me back onto the bed. "You're going to take this cock in your raw little pussy," he says in a dark voice as he puts one knee up onto the bed, "because that's where I want to blow every single load."

Oh God. Oh *God!* Part of me wants to flee, to be gone from this charade, this messed up Stockholm Syndrome relationship. But he's definitely a beast, and I must be a hell of a beauty by how turned on those words make me. They should send me running to the hills, not bending back on the bed, arching my back like a wanton slut.

But I do want it, and his dark words only excite something within me, something I've never been aware of until now. My hands go to the sides of my pants, and I tug them down, revealing myself inch by inch, showing him exactly what type of a woman I am.

He watches with those dark, smoldering eyes of his as I shed my pants, unveiling myself to his hungry eyes. His dick swells and throbs before me, the biggest I've ever seen and looking so fiercely aroused after my sucking. He yanks away my pants and panties as they reach my ankles, then grasps hold of my thighs, pressing them back, spreading me open wide as he gets between my legs.

"If you're going to be mine, you're never going to need any protection again," he rumbles, and part of me acknowledges that he means both protection from others, and protection from him knocking me up. But my brain buzzes on the latter point as he takes hold of the base of his cock and smacks it against my wet pussy lips.

It sends a jolt through me, and I cry out in pleasure, my body contorting before him. I can't stop looking at him, at the muscular Adonis who is so filled with dangerous desire. Does he want me to push him away? Does he think that's what he's doing?

Instead, he's ignited a white hot flame within me, and I lift my hips toward his dick, begging him with my wet pussy.

"You want me?" I try to purr seductively, but instead it comes out as all desire with no finesse. It'll have to do.

"I've got you," he growls, grasping the hair at the back of my head.

His chiseled body is marked with tattoos, which only adds to how fearsome he looks. But somehow, despite how commanding he is, I feel like I'm safe with him. That helps as he wields that massive shaft of his, piercing my womanhood with it as he sinks down into me with a single motion, causing me to cry out as he moans. My narrow little pussy stretched so wide to accommodate him, it hurts!

I feel so alive, so present in the moment. The sensation of his flesh against mine, the sound of his heavy breathing, the light scent of our arousal mixing in the air... It all comes together to form a cocktail of exquisite beauty, and I reach out, my nails digging into his hip. I catch a gleam of a scar just beyond my thumb, but I can't even wonder how he got it. Not now.

Now, all I concern myself with is his body crushing mine.

His powerful form goes to work, grasping me, holding me in place as he begins to piston that massive shaft into me. Deep, hard thrusts pounding to the utmost depths of my womanhood as he moans over top of me, and all that beautiful muscle glistens with rising perspiration.

He's hard, and it twinges a little, but I take him and I love it. He's rougher than before, his balls slapping against my ass noisily as the bed creaks.

And there's something hard in his eyes, something dangerous, but even that turns me on. I can't turn away from his darkness, because something in him speaks to me. His roughness complements my hidden needs, and already I'm finding my body begin to spark with electricity.

He hasn't even touched my clit, but I can feel the jolts begin to cluster there at the apex of my thighs, just above his harsh body.

This was meant to be his dominion over me, showing me what it means to be his girl. But here I am building toward an orgasm as he pumps his way to his release. And as I rub my slender fingers over his chest, feeling the ridges of hard muscle beneath, I can feel the sinew tighten, feel him approaching his own climax.

"I'll make you mine, girl," he growls huskily, watching his torso undulate as he approaches his end.

"I am yours," I gasp out, and I don't even realize what I'm saying. It's just the truth, blurted out without thought seconds before the ultimate pleasure crashes down upon me. My fingers tighten into the blankets as I scream, my body turning electric.

For a moment as pleasure explodes within me, I forget that this big, brutish hunk is about to unload inside me. And he does just that a mere moment later, his dick swelling as he lets loose a roar. His release coming on fast and hard as he pumps me full, thick gouts of his virile seed flooding into my unprotected depths, just the way he wanted, as he claims me atop the motel room bed.

He's a wild beast, taking me so roughly in those final moments as he gives me every last spurt and drop he has. The view of his rippling physique on display as he tenses, keeping himself pressed to my utmost depths.

Never in my life have I felt so free, and the irony is definitely not lost upon me. This moment, this beautiful, wonderful moment of the purest type of passion is utter perfection.

My arms wrap around him, our bodies glistening with perspiration, and I lift my head to kiss him.

He kisses me back, holding me a while, and everything seems so perfect. He's passionate and warm in the after-glow of our sex. But after I begin to drift off atop the bed with him in the late night, I feel him pull away, untangling himself from me.

"Where are you going?" I murmur with a hazy, groggy voice.

"I have to pay the price for your hideaway," he says, and just like that a chill runs through me. I know what he means.

Someone's going to die.

Chapter 13

Mikhail

Doing a hit comes as naturally to me as changing the tires on a pickup truck comes to a mechanic. It's just a simple task that comes along with the trade.

The real chore of doing a hit is all the prep work. And that's why I'm out in the pre-twilight hours of the morning, tracking down my target for the hit. It didn't take long to locate him, as rich guys live large and lavishly. A simple text to a source I've long relied on, and the address is mine. He even fishes up whether the guy is likely home or abroad. He's likely home.

I pop over to the guy's manor and get a peek at what vehicle he rides in. It requires me slipping in, balaclava and all, and this is the riskiest part. Because a fuckup here can ruin everything. But there's just the one car, which thankfully makes things easier. I know what he'll be riding in. It's a sports car, two-seater. Which narrows things down. I know he's only going to be in one of two places.

With that out of the way I slip away, the world's quietest yet least successful burglar, then get to work.

Remember that stuff about mechanics? Well, I fancy myself one part of the time, with some of the work I do. I ditch my car elsewhere in town once driving near my target, then swipe a car. It's an easy thing, stealing a car, even these expensive new ones.

It's a BMW, a model I'm used to working with. It'll work great for what I have in mind, a nice sturdy, solid hood.

I drive the car over to a closed garage. Picking locks is something I learned back in Russia as a teen, and has always come in handy. Before any time is passed I'm inside and working on my new acquisition.

My jacket's tossed aside, sleeves rolled up as I get down into the guts of the machine. I'm doing things to this beautiful car that no mechanic ever should. The person who owns this shop would probably shit himself if they saw. It won't run long when I'm finished, but it won't need to.

The only thing left is to drive over to my target's place, and wait.

Sunlight is beginning to spill over the horizon, so it won't be too bad. A good hit usually requires a lot of waiting, but I'm accelerating this contract. I want it done fast. Normally I'd never let myself rush a job, especially not on a high profile target like a rich white guy, but I want the club free of this nuisance so they can focus on helping protect my girl.

My girl.

Bozhemoi. I'm a fucking fool. Suckered in by her pretty, good looks, her creamy skin and sweet lips. Not to mention that wry sense of humor she has...

Just when I start coming to my senses, that maybe I'm

being foolish to even toy with this relationship, she slips into my mind, like I slipped into her. And I'm as paralyzed by it now as we were in the moment. The way she gave into me when I tried to discourage her, how she sought to please me instead...

That thought gets choked off when I realize how much time has passed, and the gates to the rich prick's property open up, his car pulling down the driveway. I can't afford to think of pretty little Alicia, slumbering back in the motel bed. Now, it's all business.

The car comes to life, the engine giving an uneven hum as it begins to build toward its end. *Just hold on a little longer*, I think to myself.

Luckily this guy drives like an old man. Despite living in the lap of luxury he handles his sporty vehicle like a porcelain doll. Edging into turns in a way that's painful to watch. I could almost yell at him to take advantage of that beautiful car before it's too late.

I don't want to do this in the rich part of town. Police are probably itching to come to the rescue here, and my getaway on foot will be a nightmare. So I follow this miserable fuck into the heart of the city, into the busy downtown streets. Broad daylight.

Usually a hitman hides in the shadows, under cover of night. But time is of the essence, and sometimes hiding in plain sight is the best option.

I'm holding off a nice distance; he's moving so slowly it'd be suspicious to even tail at my usual length. But I know my opportunity is going to come soon... and there it is. This prick's agonizing slowness finally pays off as he's edging around a left turn. And I have him perfectly.

I speed up, smoke licking up from beneath the hood of

this beautiful vehicle as I make out as if I'm going to rush the light. I swerve right, then left, and bam! The collision does the trick, my jury-rigging of the engine comes to fruition as the hood explodes, launching forward.

It's a gambit, I know, but my handiwork never fails. And with the right angle and speed of impact, that metal hood hits just as I hope... well, almost. It strikes the old fuck in the head, leaving a deep gash in his forehead as he jerks away.

Panic breaks out, traffic backs up. But I'm unfazed by the impact, and I get out of the vehicle.

"Hey buddy, you okay?" I ask in my best American accent, closing in on the injured target.

He's still sitting there, hurt pretty badly, blood gushing from his wound. But it's not enough. I never half-ass things or leave them to chance.

"Oh shit, someone call an ambulance," I say to the closest onlookers, making them back off and fumble with their smartphones. It gives me the time and space I need to get in close.

My target's beady eyes lock onto me, and I can feel the hatred and anger there. But he's very nearly crippled, his neck might've even broken. I reach in as if testing his pulse, but I'm feeling his spine.

Nope, not quite broken.

"Is he okay?" someone asks from a dozen feet behind me.

My leather-gloved hands take hold of that lousy prick's neck and head, and I twist. The snapping noise is loud, and I hear someone at a distance cry, "What's that?!" But I ignore it.

I release the limp man, let his head dangle loosely as I turn and begin to walk away.

"I think I'm going to be sick," I say, but my hearts not quite in the act. He's just another slime ball who had it coming. I make my way into a nearby shopping complex, head toward the bathrooms before veering off, making my way through to exit out a side door.

The job's done, and while there were unavoidable witnesses, I just look like someone who got into an accident and couldn't handle it. I'll be gone from this city in no time anyhow, and there is no trace of me in the car I was driving. I'll be nothing more than a ghost of a memory after I head back to New York.

I'll let Alicia know once I'm there.

As I peel off the bloody gloves and dispose of them in a trash can, my phone comes to life. I can't ignore it, not with the way things are, so I slip it out of my pocket.

It's Alicia.

I should turn it off, send her sweet self to my voicemail. Preserve a little memory, a glimpse of what I could have, if I were a different man, living a different life. But my gut won't let me. I never ignore my gut instinct.

"Yes?" I answer, but the panicked heavy breathing I hear on the other side already tells me what I need to know: she's in serious trouble.

CHAPTER 14

ALICIA

Hearing his voice gives me a jolt of relief. I know he's probably the last person in the world I should trust, but somehow, I know he's going to protect me. And right now, I definitely need protection.

I don't know what's happening, not really, but everything in my bones is screaming at me that something is wrong. Maybe it's my women's intuition, or the fact that the bright light of day seems so eerie. Maybe it's just that Eva's come and checked in on me twice, and not just out of boredom. She says there's nothing wrong, but there's definitely something up, and whatever it is, I'm on edge. I'm not going to pretend that it's all in my head like I did with Mr. Gallego.

I'm not going to pretend I can handle anything that comes my way. I know better than that now.

"Something's wrong," I manage as I peek out the window. All I can see are blue skies and lazy cars driving along, nothing out of the ordinary. So why is my gut screaming at me that I'm in danger?

I strain my ears, and I hear a scuffle in the next room. Is that just my neighbor or... Maybe it is all in my head. Maybe I'm just jumpy and want Mikhail back by my side and this is the only way I can do it.

"I'm on my way," he says to me with that voice that convinces me he's going to have everything under control in no time. That husk of his is the sound of a man who never lets anyone get away with anything he doesn't want them to.

Though we hang up, I creep to the door again, only to hear a loud thud from outside. Then shit starts to get very real as I peek out the door and see Eva point a gun out beneath the curtains. Gunshots go off, both hers and another, but I'm screaming, I can't help it!

"Stay down!" Eva shouts at me, but I'm already falling to my knees.

I can see only shadows move across the window through the curtains, and along the crack beneath the door. But multiple figures are beating at the door and firing shots inside.

I'm surrounded by killers, and all I've ever been is an office employee, hidden from the violence of the world. And now, I'm really regretting not taking up those self-defense courses! I've never known the depths of helplessness until now, and I edge away from the door and windows.

A bullet rips through the shitty stucco of the motel room, grazing my calf, but the weird thing is that I barely feel it, even though I'm still screaming like a maniac. Even as the blood starts to drip, it's like I'm in a daze. I look around the room, trying to find some shelter, and then I see it.

Sure, it's just a flowery, ancient ironing board, but if I can get that and block the space under the bed, it could be a makeshift shelter at least.

I just have to hold out until Mikhail gets here. That's all. He'll know how to take down these maniacs.

I rush to the closet, grabbing the ironing board. It's unwieldy, and the legs seem really rusted somehow, but it's still metal, and that's gotta be better than these thin little walls.

Someone screams next door, and then goes deathly silent, and it sends a chill through me. Was that Eva? One of my protectors?

It's only a matter of time...

I can't think of that. Not now. There's no escape, there's just survival, so I crawl in under the bed, fixing the ironing board in place.

Not a moment too soon, because I hear a bullet strike the metal board right after. Whether it did anything to deflect it from me, I can't tell, but I count myself lucky anyhow.

I curl up in a ball beneath the bed, clasping my wounded calf to stem the flow of blood. I rip some fabric from a dangling bedsheet and tie it around my leg before things go eerily quiet.

That silence is more blood curdling than the loud bangs of gunshots.

After a while I see a flicker of movement through a bullet hole in the wall. Then the door bursts open and I stifle a squeal before it can get out.

"Alicia?!" hisses Eva, looking for me.

"I'm here!" I rasp back from beneath the bed and she

looks down, gun in hand as she shuts the door and reloads her gun.

"I plugged a few of these goons," she says to me, looking primed and ready despite her disheveled state. "There's more but help should be here at any moment," she says, breathing heavily.

"Who are they?" I ask, as if it matters. They're the bad guys. The ones with guns that are shooting at me and a woman who's protecting me. "Is there anything I can do?" I ask, deciding that's a much better question.

"Just stay hidden," she says, running a hand back over her hair, "that's the smartest thing you can do." She fishes into the waistband of her jeans in back, pulling out a small revolver and a tiny black object, laying them down close to me. "Take these, hide this in your clothes, and shoot anyone who tries to take you. But for the love of God don't blow my head off if I come racing back in here!"

"R-right," I manage, staring for a second at the cold metal. I don't want to touch it. I'm scared of it, and I tremble as I reach out, wrapping my hand around the grip. I can at least use it to frighten off anyone who tries to shoot at me, right?

Regardless, it's better to have it. Makes me feel a tad stronger, now that it's in my hands.

What really helps make me feel better, though, is the roar of motorcycle engines, because judging by the look on Eva's face, help is here.

I quickly tuck the little black object into my sock, with nary a clue as to what it is or why.

"The cavalry has arrived," she says with a cocky grin. But the daring woman doesn't stop there; she bursts through the door and opens fire on the thugs after us, giving cover to her gang members as they pull up.

It doesn't take long before the roar of motorcycle engines is drowned out by gunfire, though, as an even more intense firefight breaks out.

It feels like time is moving so fast and so slowly all at once. I can't really see anything happening, as that'd defeat the purpose of hiding, but I can hear it all, and that's just as bad.

"Please, Mikhail," I whisper under my breath, trying desperately to summon him into existence. "Please hurry."

I can see the silhouettes and shadows of figures fighting outside the room, and then suddenly, there's a spray of blood right in front of me, and Eva falls to the ground, blood starting to pool beneath her.

The fighting doesn't stop, but bodies start spilling into the room outside. I hold the gun, but I can't tell if they're friend or foe, and I don't want to risk blowing away one of the gang members here to save me.

By the time heavy boots come stomping into the room and I can make out the mobbed up attire that looks nothing like what the biker gang would wear, it's too late. They easily tear apart my makeshift shelter. They've got me!

CHAPTER 15

MIKHAIL

Before the call even ended I was running. The nearest car will do, I tell myself before cracking the side window and reaching in to open the door.

The act didn't go unnoticed, but it's too late for that. I bust open the panel beneath the steering wheel and hotwire the vehicle, making it come to life in a heartbeat. There's no time for a graceful getaway now, I'll just have to trust that I've put enough distance between me and the scene of the hit to not be suspicious as I speed away.

Every moment on the road is agonizing, every second feels like an hour as my head plays out possibilities for what I'm going to return to. It takes my usual business cool to get my head back on track, to prevent all the worries of a man's infatuation from messing up my driving.

I zip between cars and lanes, take a few sharp turns and finally... I can see it.

There, at the motel, cars and motorcycles are strewn

about the parking lot as a few people lie bleeding on the ground, and gunshots ring out in the air.

I keep focused, pop open my door, and get my gun in hand. One breath, then I dive out of the car, plow the vehicle into one of the black sedans and subsequently one of the thugs inside, as well as another standing at the back.

The large crash kicks up enough of a distraction that as I roll along the ground and come to a halt, I have enough time to raise my gun and take out one of the attackers. Another goes down as I rise up then rush behind cover.

It's never been hard for me to snuff out a life. I've dealt with high-stress situations, risky hits before. It's like water off a duck's back.

But never have I let myself feel anything during a hit. Not anger, not pain, not fear. Especially not fear.

But now, it grips my heart, knowing Alicia is in there, and that she needs me. She needs me to be *me*. She needs me to be at my best, but my heart and mind are clouded with something else, all the emotions that I've forgotten I even knew how to feel.

It's going to make me careless if I don't push them aside. I have to, for her.

Get my head back in the game. Focus. Concentrate.

She needs me, damn it, and I'm not going to let my girl down.

I rise up and fire a couple shots in the direction of the shooters up on the higher level before making a dash to the stairs. They weren't shots intended to hit, just distract, as I made my way in. The cover fire from the gang members that are here to help also aids me as I move, avoiding taking any bullets myself.

The stairs are tricky, because I know some of these guys

are waiting for me at the top, ready to blow my head off the moment it peeks above the railing as I climb the stairs. So I have to do something else. I can't wait.

I could go through one of the rooms here, come out the other side, climb through the window and up onto the next level, taking them by surprise. But that would take a whole lot of time I don't have if I'm going to get to Alicia.

A quick study of my surroundings shows I don't have many options, but I take what I have.

There's a pole directly above me, pointing out horizontally. Looks like it once sported signage for the motel, but the sign itself must've been removed by vandals long ago. It's metal, but there's no way of telling if it could support my weight.

All the same I jump for it with one hand, grasp hold of that pole and dangle there. Exposed. It's a foolish move, and I only hope that their surprise is enough to save my ass. I can support myself with one arm easily enough, I've been keeping myself in peak condition for so long. The real weakness is in the sign pole, and on whether I can lift my gun up and take aim fast enough.

I see the two thugs immediately through the railing above. One doesn't see me right away, but the other in back does.

I'm not motionless, so it takes a moment longer than usual to raise my gun and aim it right. In that time the pale dirt bag gets a chance to whip his own gun toward me. He fires first, but my bullet's just a fraction of a second behind.

Fate's sealed either way.

I'm hit, and I feel the bullet tear through my arm, the only thing holding me up. It's like molten fire, but I don't lose my grasp, it's iron solid. I know it's a grazing hit. I won't let it take me down, not with her on the line.

The other guy, however? With a bullet straight through his left eye, he goes down and I'm able to take my second shot. Adrenaline courses through me, and I know I'll get the girl. This is what I was born to do, what I was meant to do.

I'm a killing machine, and now that my head's in the game, not even a bullet can take me back out of it.

I fire at the other guy as I let myself drop to the ground. He fires too, but he aims where I was, not where I am now. A moment later, I hit the pavement as I hear something move above. I can't tell what happened to the guy, but I trust in my aim and sprint up the stairs on foot. Blood splatters from my arm onto the steps and as I turn, gun ready, I see the two men are both down. My aim was true.

As I rush toward Alicia's broken door and see the shattered glass, my heart ices over. I leap through the glass and prepare myself to take on her assailants, but when I see a woman's body on the floor and blood, my own vision turns red.

"Alicia!" I growl the name out in a bellowing shout as I surge into the bedroom toward the body. But it's not her. It's Eva.

The woman's eyes flutter open as I look around the room, see the mess of the place, the ironing board and items strewn about, the blood staining the carpet and smearing toward the door.

"Get her..." Eva says weakly.

She's burning up and badly wounded, but she should survive. I hope. They didn't get her in the gut or any of the vitals, at least, so as long as the ambulance gets here quickly enough she'll be alright. With a motel like this, I imagine there's been at least a few calls in about the gunfight in the parking lot, so I give her a nod and a pat on the shoulder.

But I don't know how to take her advice. There's no sign of Alicia, and the room is in such a mess, it's impossible to figure out what happened. There's only one exit, though, and it's the door I came in through, so I take a step toward it just before a scream pierces the air.

I only get a fraction of a moment's time before a bullet whips past my head and I have to duck down, but I spot Alicia, being dragged through the parking lot.

I run back out of the motel room and race around the side of the building towards the back lot. Her blood is marking the way, and it's making my body scream in anger, but I can't let it distract me. I need to push it down, into my fist, let it make me hard. For so long, I've honed my body and my mind to be cold and ruthless, but now I'm burning hot with rage, and it's a new sensation entirely.

The back parking lot is smaller and there's only one car there, and just two guys. One pushing Alicia into the back of the car and another pointing his gun right at me.

The shot goes off as I dive forward, losing precious moments. But it saves my life, in two ways.

Not only do I dodge that shot from the goon below, but the third thug that's rounding the corner with his gun held high instead finds me at his feet. In the seconds I have, I manage to twist and grab hold of his wrist, keeping the gun pointed away from me as I raise my own weapon and fire.

But my position's not optimal on the floor like this and

he's able to grab my wrist as I did to him, and my shot misses his ugly mug by an inch or so. It comes down to a battle of raw strength, but I have the guys down below to worry about, too. I don't have the time to fight him over this, not if I'm going to save Alicia from the other guys.

I hear doors slam shut, and thankfully no more bullets, but that only makes matters more urgent. I push up from my place on the pavement, and as I rise, I'm able to put more of my strength into overpowering this guy. I'm able to stare into his scarred face as he gnashes his teeth at me.

And I recognize him. He's no ordinary goon, he's from Brighton Beach. He's one of Vasili's men. And that makes me realize the guy in the gaudy suit below, the one that shoved her into the car was Vasili himself.

"The girl's ours," he says to me with a sneer, and I bash his nose in with a vicious head-butt, sending a spray of blood all over the both of us. That's all I need to get my gun pointed back at his face and blow an inch wide hole through his skull.

I rise up, wiping the blood from my face and eyes so I can see, but the image that greets me fills me with rage. The black sedan is pulling away out of the parking lot, with the image of Alicia in the back window looking at me, panic in her emerald eyes.

I raise my gun to try and shoot out one of their back tires, but their erratic movements, the distance, my blood-blurred vision, and Alicia's precarious position at the rear of the vehicle mean it's a shot I can't risk taking.

Instead I watch in horror as my girl is hauled off by Vasili. A sick, sadistic bastard whose only intent will be to torture her to get her to incriminate me to Gregorovich, and then murder her.

Chapter 16

Alicia

I can't see where I am anymore. At some point, I'm not entirely sure when, they got sick of my screaming after watching Mikhail vanish in the rear-view mirror. The one cruel thug forced a gag in my mouth and a sack over my head. It felt like hours ago that happened, but I'm no longer sure of time or pretty much anything else, either.

I was trying to memorize the turns, as if that'd help me instruct Mikhail if I ever got to talk to him again, but I long ago lost count. It certainly didn't help that it felt like we kept veering off the road and driving erratically. It's any wonder we didn't get pulled over, but then I guess there's not a lot of cops wherever they're taking me.

I just know that as we get to the end of the journey, they're hauling me out of the backseat and I feel my feet dragging over cement once we're inside. Which means we're not in some cozy place. We're probably in some dank, abandoned factory. The kind of place people end up right before they get shot by the mob.

The kind of place I never even knew to dread dying in.

This isn't the life I ever could have expected for myself, not by a long shot, but now I suppress a sob. That's all the bit of pride I can muster, to at least meet my death with some grace and dignity.

"Tie her to the bed," says the snarling voice of the man who hauled me into his car, the cruel little goblin of a man.

There goes the last bit of my resolve, and I'm screaming again. I can handle the idea of being killed, my body never found, my mom left to mourn a daughter she doesn't know is dead. I could, at least, make peace with that.

But being put on a bed by these goons, I know that spells trouble of a far greater magnitude, and fear jolts through me. I struggle, my arms nearly torn from their sockets as I yank against them, but they're both taller and stronger than me by quite a lot.

What greets me isn't the soft cushioning of a bed, however, not even the rough fabric of some dingy old mattress. It's just hard metal springs of a bare bed frame digging into me as I'm pushed onto it and stretched out.

I've never felt so degraded and so terrified all at once. Every last bit of me wants to scream but my voice is hoarse. I can barely even breathe, and the throbbing of my bullet wound seems even worse now. I don't know if it's all in my head or what, but every part of me aches, like I'm being pulled apart.

"Shaddup!" screams the voice of that cruel one, the leader, right before he hits me across the face, knocking the feeble sounds from my lips.

As I sputter and cough from the blow, the two men tie me up so tightly that my poor wrists feel like they're being sawed through by the rope. Every part of me is either in pain or in extreme discomfort, and I find myself just wishing I could disappear into the ground and be back home.

But when the word comes to mind — home — it isn't my apartment I'm picturing. It's Mikhail's safehouse. Boring, bland, and filled with such red hot lust and passion I can barely contain myself. My home is him, now.

"Let me go," I beg, almost sobbing the words out. But for my misery the leader yanks my hood off, ripping a few hairs from my head in the process.

"I said shut up!" he shouts, and I'm looking up at his beady-eyed face, so wild with anger, his hand garnished with a ton of glittering gemmed-rings upon it, poised and ready to hit me. "You speak when I tell you to, *da*?" he asks, getting up in my face, grinding his teeth.

I turn away from him, able to see around the building I'm in. I notice weird details about it, like how it's not an abandoned factory as I thought, just some near-empty warehouse. I try to drink it all in, memorize every inch of it, just in case.

Just in case you discover telepathy? My inner voice asks, and I don't even have the energy to fight back. I'm going to die here, and this disgusting man's beady eyes are going to be the last thing I see.

But I guess instinct kicks in, some sense of self preservation, because I nod. I can't die in here, and I'm going to do whatever I need to in order to survive.

That glaring troll grabs my face and twists me toward him, his own lips curled in an almost freakish manner.

"Tell me who was protecting you, huh? Who saved your ass from the hotel that night?!" He screamed that last question at me, trying to intimidate me in his pinstripe suit with his fist in the air.

I shouldn't be so surprised by the question, but I am, and it takes me a second to even realize what he's asking. He wants me to incriminate Mikhail, to say something against him. I don't know why, but I guess it's because he protected me, and that these were the guys that he'd warned me about. It sends a shiver down my spine, but I shake my head.

"I don't know! I blacked out!" I say, and it's truthful enough. I just hope I sound honest saying it.

"Don't lie to me!" he screams at me, grabbing hold of my hair and wrenching my head forward to the limits of my bindings. "Tell me who it was!" he bellows, pulling out a knife from his pants pocket.

I feel like I'm going to be sick, even though I haven't eaten in a long time. I can't help it, I just start coughing, my stomach constricting with how scared I am. I've never been so afraid in all my life, and I beg myself just to tell him, to give him Mikhail's name, but I know I could never do that!

I've fallen hard for my former kidnapper, and I know he was trying to save me. I saw him, wanting to protect me again from these thugs. How could I betray him after all we've been through?

Tears sting my eyes as my retching subsides, but I keep shaking my head. I don't know when the words start spilling out, over and over, but I'm aware of myself saying, "I don't know, it's the truth," over and over again.

"You're lying!" he screams at me again and pushes the knife up into my face, letting the metal cut into my cheek, cold and piercing. "Just give me his name! It's that *zasranec* Mikhail, isn't it?! Just say it!"

My body is in anguish, begging me to just tell him. Let

Mikhail's name tumble from my lips, and let this all be over. Maybe he'll even just let me go, even after all of this, if I just obey. But I can't pretend I'm even considering it.

There's no way I'm going to betray Mikhail. There's no way I'm going to turn my back on my only real chance at love.

It's like suddenly everything he told me kicks into place. The reason why Mikhail had been so cold and distant, the reason he felt he needed to protect me. I now know he wasn't bluffing just to keep me in place.

He's been honest to me this entire time, and my heart thuds with fear and love, the emotions mingling into a twisted warmth. I'm going to get out of this. I'm going to survive so that I can tell him that he was right.

"I have no idea! I was drugged!"

Then I hear it, a voice coming in a little tinny. My abuser is looking at the phone upon a nearby box as the voice rises out of it. It's all in a foreign language I don't understand, Russian I think, but one name stands out from all the talk: Mikhail.

My captor speaks back, but suddenly all his anger and venom is gone and he has such deference in his voice. It doesn't last long, though, before his full attention is back upon me as rage flares up in his eyes.

"I am going to give you one last fucking chance to tell the truth," he says with barely contained anger. "And if you don't tell me what I want, then I am going to start cutting off fingers," he says, and he grabs hold of my hand, which is by now already partly numb, twisting my finger so hard I hear a crack and cry out in pain.

It's like a lightning bolt through my brain, and I can barely even think. All that remains is pain and hurt, and even when I try to squirm, the jagged springs of the bed prod my back and offer no relief.

Tears flood my eyes and I feel them dripping into my hair, but I shake my head. My voice trembles, my mouth filled with saliva and making it harder to talk. "Please stop. I don't know anything!"

"That's it," he growls and he presses the blade into my finger and I see blood well up. "You brought this on yourself," he declares, working on severing my index finger.

CHAPTER 17

MIKHAIL

For the first time in my life since I was but a boy, I find myself at a loss. There are no other cars in the back lot to steal, and going back around front to get something to take, and then to navigate around to meet the speeding Vasili, would take far too long.

It's all falling apart before me.

But I have to try, and I turn and run back all the same, because I won't give up. That's not who I am. I'm no quitter. However, the sight of Eva stumbling out of the room, clutching her side gives me pause.

"Wait," she says, and I stop to help her.

"Will you make it? I have to go and try to rescue her, I can't afford to stop," I tell her, because as much as I want to help this brave woman out, Alicia's life is forfeit if I don't find her as soon as possible.

"Don't worry about me," she says, fishing into her pocket and pulling out a phone. "I gave her my GPS tracker," she says, opening her phone and activating the tracking app before handing it to me. "Go get her," she says with grim determination on her blood spattered face.

I pause, thankfulness welling up in me for what this woman has done. I want to ask her one last time if I can help, but I see already two of her gang coming up the stairs toward us.

"I'll bring her back safe and sound," I pledge.

"You better," Eva tells me.

I head back to my stolen ride as the sounds of sirens slowly filter toward us. We all need to get the hell out of here soon, regardless, unless we want the police to screw everything up for us.

I run my fingers through my hair as I tear out of the parking lot, then instantly force myself to slow down. I'm not going to do her any good by getting the attention of the cops. Especially after clamping my hand down on the wheel and seeing the trail of blood down around my forearm. I'd completely forgotten I'd been shot.

I put the wheel between my knees as I tear at the bottom of my shirt, ripping a strip off and wrapping it around my wound. I'll need to get fixed up later, probably a couple stitches, but for now, this'll do. I flex my hand, testing to see how much mobility I have, and find that the shooter must've missed every important nerve. I still have full range of motion, and that's good, because I'll need it. Still, I've lost a lot of blood, and I can feel the effects. My reaction time won't be at its peak.

I glance at the little beeping GPS tracker, and I can tell I'm getting closer. It's not pinpoint accuracy, but it's close enough. Eventually I track Vasili to the industrial part of town, and there's only so many options for him to hold someone hostage.

Or murder someone...

I shake my head free of the thought. I saved her once from my own wrath, and now I'm going to save her from Vasili's torturous little hands.

Finally I come upon the black sedan I was looking for, parked alongside an old warehouse, but across from another. It's one of the two, but my bet is on Vasili being too lazy and stupid to take even the slightest bit of care in hiding his destination.

I pull to a stop down the road slowly, so I won't be overheard approaching. Getting out of the car though, I nearly stumble. I'm lightheaded from the loss of blood, more so than I anticipated. It'll be a tough time making up for it, but there's no turning away from it now. Not when my girl's life is on the line.

I do my best to focus myself, push away the daze, but it's not something easily done. The light-headedness from blood loss isn't a pain I can simply push past, it's something at a base level, beyond my control. I can't ignore it, because ignoring it lets it control me. Best I can do is try and compensate for it, take into consideration the way it affects my movements, the loss of focus.

Making my way to the door I try to keep my senses peeled. Vasili isn't a mob boss, and the number of guys he had at the motel was big. It must've been every thug he had under his thumb, and maybe a few extra he paid for the occasion. Which likely meant it was just down to him and that one guy he has with him.

Two on one are not odds I'm afraid of, generally speaking. I take on much worse as usual business. But with my head like this, it's a risk. A big one. And if I fuck this up, it'll be both Alicia's and my life.

I take out my gun, a little later than I should've, and check the clip. Only a few rounds, but more than enough to get this job on a regular day.

Approaching the door I stop and I peek in through a grated window to get the best view I can, but the grime on the glass makes it difficult. Still, I can see a bit of movement to the left hand side, and I'd bet it's them.

Even through the glass, though, I can hear a high pitched scream, muffled by the building.

My heart pounds, but I try to calm myself down. That's a good sign. It means she's alive, if nothing else. Pain means living.

Life is pain.

And as the stabbing, throbbing pain in my arm attests, as long as you're alive and feeling that pain, you can still fight.

I kick in the door and lift my gun, firing off an initial shot at one of the men. It misses. I never miss. The damn light-headedness is messing with me. I pop off another shot as the thug spins around to aim his own gun at me, and this time he goes down.

"Mikhail," Alicia gasps, her poor body tied up to a bed frame, and I can see there's blood on her clothes. I can't focus on that. Right now, I just have to worry about keeping her safe.

"Fuck!" Vasili screams. I didn't know who I was taking out at first, my vision not as clear as I'm used to like this. But I'd recognize that weasely voice anywhere, any time. "Don't move or I'll—" I pop off another shot that takes Vasili in the shoulder or arm, I can't tell. He goes down all the same. *I'm not going to play some point-less standoff with this prick, if I wimp out and don't take the shot, he has all the control, and then Alicia and I are both dead.*

I can't finish him off at this angle, because the bed is obscuring my view and Alicia is in the line of fire now. So I have to advance on them.

My walk isn't the usual intimidating stride, I'm wobbling a little, I realize, even if I can't quite feel it. I'm not going to be able to keep up this fight much longer, my reaction times are horrible, my aim is off, and this guy — as awful as he is — will gain the advantage on me with time.

"Come out," I bellow at him, my voice thankfully losing none of its aggressive growl, at least.

"Fuck you!" he says as he reaches an arm up over the foot of the bed to shoot at me. I fire first, but it misses. He fires.

A miss.

I fire again and hit his forearm, making him scream and curse as he flails away. Alicia is still tied to the bed, but I'm close enough now that I don't need to worry about hitting her, even with my aim as off as it is.

"You're over, snake," I say, pointing my gun straight down at his face, his panicked expression, hair matted to his sweaty forehead undaunting me. I pull the trigger and…

Nothing.

I'm out.

Normally I'd never lose count in a fight like this, but it's all I can do to keep things straight. I pull the trigger again to make sure. Nothing.

Vasili's face turns from abject terror to amusement, and he laughs at me.

"You fucked u—" he starts to shout, but as woozy as I am, I still manage to turn the gun around and beat him across the face with the handle in one smooth move. Some of Vasili's teeth go flying from his mouth in a spray of blood.

I don't waste energy on words, I grab hold of his expensive shirt and coat with my injured arm, and continue to beat him with the right. Hard blows upon meat and bone, his jaw cracking as I hammer away. While the blood might've drained out of me to an unhealthy degree, it's blood in my view as I exact the price for fucking with my girl.

No amount of pain or suffering will make up for his terrorizing Alicia. I just need to make sure he never lives another moment to possibly trouble her.

It's not until his face is misshapen and shattered that I hear Alicia crying out, her words a garbled mess, marked with sobs and rage. "Fucking kill him," she hisses before she slumps back, exhausted. But even still, she's a fighter, trying to work off the tight rope that's no doubt cutting into her skin.

She can't wait to be rid of this place, and neither can I.

With a final bloody blow to Vasili's face, I knock him down to the concrete floor and raise my booted foot. I slam the heel down into his head and hear his neck snap.

The rat deserved no better death, and I'm only too happy to give it to him.

I look over at Alicia, and find her staring down at the gory mess, clutching one of her hands. The rope has rubbed her wrists raw, she must've struggled free a little, but that doesn't explain the blood dripping from her fist. For a second, I think she's going to be sick, so I shield her from Vasili's corpse, from the sight that she never should've had to witness.

My arms wrap around her body and tug her close, protecting her for just a second from all the evils of the world. But I can't protect her from me.

"We have to get out of here," I murmur toward her ear, hoping that I don't frighten my sweet Alicia. I take a moment to swipe the car keys from Vasili's corpse as she nods against my chest. Even though when she stands, she trembles like a leaf.

I remove the rest of her bindings, then help her up. We step around the bodies, her face buried into my ribs the entire way out.

I'm not about to take the stolen car any further, and Vasili's should be safe, so I help Alicia into the passenger side before starting up the vehicle. This is sloppy work, and I've left a trail from one crime scene to another with the stolen vehicle left behind, but now I have to concern myself with *her* safety, not mine.

"Where are we going?" she asks me in a wavering voice, trembling with hurt and anxiety. I want to hold her, tell her everything will be alright, but there's no time. We have to be long gone from here before anyone comes by. Police or mob.

"I'll take you to my nearest safehouse," I tell her in a firm, hard voice.

"You have more than one?" she asks, and I'm glad that thought at least distracts her from the situation. It's enough to make me laugh, if only just a bit.

"*Da*, I do," I say, shooting her a sidelong confident look. "A real man has to be prepared for all eventualities. One safehouse is easily discovered."

She nods, still coddling her hand. I nod at it, then look in her eyes. She shakes her head.

"I'm fine. It'll just need a Band-Aid or two when we get back," she says, though I'm not sure if she's lying. I don't bother waiting to see, and instead pull back out onto the road, moving smoothly through the streets.

"I'll be the judge of that," I promise her, and even though my heart is thudding in my chest, I've never been so relieved in my life.

I have her back. She's safe. And that *Zasranec* is dead.

My nearest safehouse isn't too far out of town, and speeding as I am we get there before long. I know how to avoid the police after all, so it's no worry. The big concern is making sure the car won't be found and lead anyone to us. I take it into the garage beneath the building, into a secure little semi-private area.

Hopping out, I go around back and remove the license plate. I'll bring down an extra from the safehouse later, but for now I just tuck it beneath my arm and go to help Alicia out, opening her door and pulling her into my arms.

"It's all okay now, my *kotika*," I tell her in a reassuring tone.

And she doesn't want to be away from me, not even for a step. As I lead her up the gray stairwell she's clinging to me, holding on for dear life. We make it to the top and I unlock the metal door, but it's not until we're inside and I've locked the door once more behind us that she finally eases up.

"Is that what you were warning me would happen?" she says, her voice a bit choked up. "I never should have disobeyed you and forced you to let me out."

Her eyes are watery and the tears are about to flow, but

I wrap my arms around her, squeeze her, unable to help noticing how tiny she feels. Smaller than usual, so bunched up and troubled.

"You had no way of understanding how severe this all is," I tell her, and it's the truth. "This isn't your world you've stumbled into, it's mine. I never wanted you to experience life like this." That's the truth, too.

Her good hand goes to my cheek, and I feel her push up on tiptoe until her mouth grazes against mine, but then she winces away in pain.

"C'mon," I tell her. "Let's get your wounds looked at before we do something stupid."

Unfortunately, both of us had more than our fair share of wounds, but within thirty minutes, I've sewn us both up. She was right, thankfully, and the cut on her finger didn't drive too deeply at all. I must've interrupted him in the act of slicing off my precious *kotika's* finger.

I'd never have forgiven myself if I'd been a moment late...

I don't know which was worse, though: patching her up or taking care of my own bullet wound. A swig of alcohol numbs some of the pain, but certainly not all of it. Good thing I have steady hands and the willpower of a Minotaur.

"I need a shower," Alicia says, and I want to tell her that she shouldn't, but those emerald eyes are begging me not to. "Will you come with me? I don't want to be alone..."

I nod, "Let me run the shower for you."

I lead her down the halls, letting her look around. It's another simple place, not too dissimilar to the safehouse I'd had her in before. It's over top of a warehouse, in what was at one point undoubtedly the office section, with a break room, kitchen, lockers and shower. All of that now converted into another Spartan hideaway.

I start the water, get it nice and hot because that's the way every woman I've ever known prefers it, then I turn, only to find her there waiting for me.

"Come here," I beckon, my hands going to her top, carefully removing her blouse. I'm trying to play the gentleman, but it's hard to ignore the pillowy mounds of breast flesh barely contained in her bra. Those luscious tits are enough to steal any man's focus.

And it's impossible to take my eyes away when her breath quickens, her breasts rising faster and fuller as I look at her. I swear, I see a flush go across her creamy skin, and when I look at her face once more, she's drawn her lip into her mouth, chewing on it.

"I didn't know if I'd ever see you again," she confesses, taking a light step toward me, clearly favoring her unshot leg.

I'm woozy from the loss of blood, but I'm still made of flesh, and when her finger trails down my chest, the last thing I'm thinking about is my desire to have a shower and clean up. With her, I want to get down and dirty in every conceivable manner.

"You didn't trust in me?" I ask, my voice tinged with a hint of darkness. I hope it's enough to whet her appetite.

"I hoped I could," she says, her voice just barely above a whisper. It's nearly drowned out by the pitter patter of water beside us, the steam quickly working its way into the air. "But I thought maybe I've been too much trouble. Maybe you wanted to get rid of me after all."

I shake my head, possessiveness burning in my veins. I

keep pushing her away, so I know she's partially in the right to feel the way she does, but the idea that she couldn't trust me to rescue her burns me.

I know now what I have to do. I have to prove to her that she's mine, and there's no escaping that, or me. Not even through death.

CHAPTER 18

ALICIA

I don't know what's gotten into me. My head is spinning like a top, my body is aching all over, and all I can think of is my desire for this man. He saved me, again. And he didn't just save me, but he showed me what he is, who he is.

He's a man I should be terrified of, a man I should be running away from, but I'm not. Instead I'm standing here, wanting him to take me. To push my body to the limits and really make me feel what it is to be his woman.

My fingers trail down his body, and he simply breathes in evenly, as if he's not affected, but I know he is. I know he wants me just as badly as I want him. It's written all over his face, all over the way he can't help but stare at my semi-exposed body.

I reach into his pants, stroking him through the cotton of his trunks, and already he's as hard as a rock, pulsing with life and excitement. Whatever blood he's lost, he's got plenty to spare for this manhood of his.

"You should be careful, *kotika*," he says in that perfect voice of his, and I shake my head.

"I don't want to be careful," I reply. "I've been careful all my life. I've done the right things, gone to school. I thought I was a bad girl for drinking a bit too much a couple times, and look where that all landed me. In the lap of some sleaze bag who intended on..." I stop. I can't even bring myself to say what my boss must've planned for me by drugging me. I did my best not to reflect on it all this time, and I certainly don't want to dwell on it now.

"That doesn't mean you should lie with the devil," he says, but he doesn't move to stop the rubbing of my hand. In fact, he throbs harder as my emotions spill out of my mouth.

"Well it's too late for that, isn't it, Mikhail? We didn't intend to get wrapped up in one another's lives, but we made our choices, and I'm not going to turn my back on them now. I'm not going to pretend that what we have isn't real."

"And what is it you think we have?"

He stumps me, and I look up at him, meeting his intense gaze. I draw my lip into my mouth as I take a step closer to him.

"We don't need to talk about this. I just want you to take me," I say, and it's like unleashing a beast within him.

"Be careful what you wish for, *Kotika*," he growls as his hands quickly strip me of the rest of my clothes. It's hungry, filled with longing and power, and I'm a doll, submitting to his whims. The warm steam caresses my curves, and leaves his chest looking glossy. It makes his muscles look even more pronounced, and I can't help but purr in delight.

But when he picks me up and places me in the shower, the hot water splashing off my body, it's so much more intense. I've never showered with someone else, certainly no one like Mikhail. He strips off the rest of his clothes, peeling away the blood-spattered suit and shirt, letting me see the rippling hard muscle beneath. He's a dark Adonis, tattoos and scars upon rippling musculature. No one would ever use the word 'flawless' to describe him with the marks of hard living all over his glistening flesh, but that's how I feel looking at him like this; all naked and hard for me, and I've never wanted anyone or anything so badly in all my life.

All my concerns and fears are washed away by the steamy spray, and when he steps in, joining me, I suddenly feel small and vulnerable. For a moment, I'm lost in a trance as I watch water run down his flesh, beading along his skin as it trickles through the grooves and valleys of his bulging biceps and pecs.

I never realized how much I enjoy that feeling of powerlessness when I'm with Mikhail. For anyone else, I'd hate it. I've always been a bit standoffish, keeping people at a distance so that I can always feel in control. Everything about him reminds me that I'm not, though, and I love it.

From the simple touch of his big, hard hands, rough from a life of violence, but put to use stroking my smooth, tender flesh, to when he bends me over and the swollen crown of his cock presses against my pussy.

"Is this what you want?" he teases me, rubbing the throbbing crown of his manhood over my slickened flower.

I nod, my hand going to the wall to brace myself.

"Fuck me, Mikhail," I plead, my voice warbling. All the sounds feel so much louder and more encompassing in the small bathroom, and I can hear his breathing surround me. The shower is small, and we're pressed together. I can't escape, even if I wanted to.

"Even after you saw what I did?"

It surprises me that he'd even be concerned about something like that. Mikhail rescued me. That bastard was torturing me, and he got what was coming to him. But Mikhail's worrying about me makes my heart flutter.

Is this what love feels like? Like surrendering yourself to someone else and exposing your vulnerabilities to one another? Is it this sensation of growing soft and intense all at once? Is love bending to the scariest man you've ever met and never feeling safer?

The thought nearly blows me onto my ass, but my need is too intense. If this is love, then I want to feel it all. I want to feel him fucking me deep and hard. I want him to make me his.

"I want you," I say, my hand going to his, pulling it to my breast, making him squeeze. "I want you rough," I add on, and immediately, his fingers tighten around my nipple, tugging it. It sends a jolt through me, and it's so delicious that I moan and he thrusts his cock into me, splitting my tight folds open around his girth with one forceful motion.

There's no teasing, not this time. He's as deep as I can take him, his breath hot on my ear.

"You like it hard?"

I nod. It's something I've never told anyone else, but he's brought it out in me. Not only do I like it, but I crave it.

"Use your words, *kotika*," he says as he twists my nipple again, his other hand holding me in place.

"I like it hard," I whimper out, and he rewards me with a crack against my ass. I feel pain in so many parts, but that slap on my butt is something altogether different. It's exciting and sensual and sharp. It draws my thoughts and body into the present, making me really feel his body as it pounds against mine.

"You like taking me raw?"

I start to nod again, but then I remember his words, and I swallow. "I love it," I gasp out, and I know how risky it all is, but with Mikhail, the taboo is all the more enticing. And by how he throbs to even greater size within me, I know he loves it too.

"I'm going to pound you full of my come," he promises, his deep, rough voice containing the slightest hint of a moan. My pussy throbs with desire, with want, and I squirm against him. I want him deep, so I bend forward a little more.

"You're so bad," I whisper, and his fingers go into my hair, making me arch my back as he tugs. His mouth touches against my cheek before his teeth grab my ear, pulling upon it.

"You like your men bad."

"I like *you* bad."

"No one is ever going to take you from me again," he says into my ear, nibbling along the outer rim. "If anyone tries, they'll end up just like Vasili. You're mine, and once I knock you up and put a ring on that finger, everyone will know."

I gasp at those words, and the way he fucks me harder as he says them. All that hard, coiled muscle that so easily ended men's lives put to use hammering me, making my ass quake, making me struggle to keep steady under his assault. Those hands of his hold my hair taut, and he squeezes my tit as he takes possession of me.

"I am never letting you go now," he growls into my ear loudly as his thrusts drown out softer words. "Any offer to let you go is rescinded, *kotika*, you're mine. Now and forever," he declares, slapping my ass again, harder this time, making me cry out. His powerful hands make their every touch and squeeze felt upon my flesh.

He's like fire, marking me wherever he touches, wherever his flesh presses into mine, burning himself into me, and I love it.

His words, dark as they are, excite me, and my pussy tightens around his cock, begging him to do just that. To come in me, to mark me inside and out once more. Every thrust brings me closer to oblivion, but when his hand frees my breast and instead moves to my throbbing clit, I cry out. My knees are quaking, and the way he's rubbing me... I'm bound to lose control.

But his firm hand is on my hip, holding me up, protecting me from falling and giving me a silent permission to come all over his dick.

"That's it," he growls, and though he's still hammering me hard, I can feel myself tightening up around his dick, his manhood swelling within me in return, the sheer tightness of our mutual grasp slowing his pace. "You're going to come on my cock, and I'm going to plant a seed in your belly that'll mark you as mine for all to see," he says, his voice rising into a louder and louder roar with each new thrust.

"Come for me!" he bellows, and I feel him swell again, that shaft straining to such an impossible size within me.

It's too much. Even if I wanted to, I can't hold back a second longer, and as he thrusts into me a final time, I'm crashing over the edge into eternity. It's bliss. It's stupid, passionate, over-the-top bliss in a way I never knew a woman could feel. I had no idea sex could be like this, but he's opened me up to something new and different, and there's no going back.

Not now, not ever. Not from his body, not from his deadly hands, not from the way he makes me feel.

He's made me into someone I never knew I could be, someone I'm actually happy to be. So maybe he just found the real me and teased it to the surface.

Whatever he did, I'm left panting and squealing as he pounds into me, making me take every inch of his cock as he shoots his seed into me.

He holds nothing back, thrusting against me even as his cock remains lodged deep within me, pounding me against the wall as he groans and moans. That big, hard column of velvety steel blowing thick, creamy ropes of come deep into my waiting depths.

We both lose all grasp of words and language, lost to our pleasured moans as the lust boiling within our veins explodes into such passion, until at last, his dick spurts its remainder within me, and he's pressing me flatly between the shower wall and his hard chest.

"Good girl," he husks into my ear before kissing me softly, the water still flowing hotly around us even as his thick girth remains lodged deep within me.

His tenderness is so welcome after our rough sex, and I nuzzle into him, enjoying his praise. It's strange to have seen so many different sides of this man, sides I'm sure he's never shown anyone else. And I know he's seen parts of me that I've kept hidden.

"Mikhail," I whisper, but my word is lost to the pitter patter of the shower, the warm water washing us clean of what we've just done.

The roughness of our lovemaking flows so seamlessly into the tender embrace we share now, like the water that runs over our flesh. His thick arms wrapping around me, his mouth finding mine, only the coarseness of his stubble adding any roughness to the moment as his tongue delves deep into my mouth.

We stand like that for so long in the shower, until finally, he softens enough to tug easily from my folds, and he reaches over, grasping some soap and bringing it to my shoulder blades. This killer's tender, loving hands carefully work away the sweat, blood, and dirt of the hardest day in my life so far.

"Thank you," I murmur, and he smiles at me, as if he weren't wiping away the stains of my torture. He acts so pure, so innocent, even though I know he's not. He's a cold-blooded killer, after all. But he's more than that too, isn't he?

He takes hold of my arms, so thin and slender compared to his thick forearms and bulging biceps. With such tender care, he cleans my rope-burnt wrists, peppering my lips and face with kisses as he moves from one appendage to the other, slowly taking care to clean me from top to bottom. Cupping my breasts one at a time, soaping them up and rinsing away the foam.

Then at last, when he's done and he seeks to bring the soap to his own body, I interrupt him. Reaching out to wriggle my slender fingers into his grasp and take the bar of soap to do for him what he did for me.

It's not purely selfless. I love the way his ribbed muscles press into my soapy fingers, and I feel out the deep crevices and beautiful hills of his body. He's masculine perfection, his body honed in that gym where we first made love, and on the job where he's saved my life repeatedly, and I'm fascinated by him.

Even as the water grows cooler and goosebumps arise on both our bodies, we don't want to part. We don't want anything to disturb this perfect, tranquil moment that's stretched out between us. He takes the brunt of the cold on his back as my fingers trail down, finding his masculinity, letting the soap cleanse him of my feminine scent.

Despite our recent lovemaking and the chill water spraying his backside, he stiffens in my grasp. That hefty cock in my palm throbbing bigger, thicker, its veiny surface expanding until at last, he's more than clean and he shuts off the shower.

"Here," he says, reaching out of the shower to pluck up a towel and wrapping it around me. He's still dripping, but he picks me up in his arms, carrying me out of the bathroom and into the bedroom nearby. He doesn't give a damn about the trail of water we leave behind, but he lays me down on the edge of the bed and slowly towels me off before using it on himself. And I get the added joy of watching him stand before me, half-erect, wiping away glistening moisture from his ripped physique.

It feels like the calm after a storm, everything feeling so electric and fresh, and when he tosses the towel aside, I reach for him. I want to feel his weight on mine, to become one again.

"You're gorgeous," I say as I look him up and down, drinking in his scars, his beautiful tattoos, his rugged masculinity. I want to lick him all over, to taste his clean flesh, to make him feel good.

He places one knee upon the bed then lifts me up, laying me down in the middle of the mattress before lowering himself over me. Despite all that thick, hard muscle weighing him down, he holds himself up with ease, kissing my lips, my face, my neck, letting his free hand roam over my breasts and torso.

This time, unlike our rough and hard fuck in the shower, he's gentle and slow, even though I feel his dick so hard and pulsating, pressing along my smooth inner thighs. Mikhail's rock-hard and throbbing with need for me again already, but he takes his time, exploring my newly cleansed body as if discovering it for the first time all over again.

I feel naked, but not in the physical way, even though I am. It's like he's reached into my core and sees me as I really am, all the flaws I try to hide, and simply accepts them. Usually, being naked comes with a sense of vulnerability, but he makes it feel something so much deeper than that.

I watch as his tongue trails along my hip bone, leaving a little roadway of saliva that quickly dries away, and then he kisses closer to my sex and I shiver. I'm already so sensitive from my earlier orgasm, and now, he's so near to the source of that torturous delight.

Mikhail fucked me. Came in me. Then cleaned me again. And now here he is, his lips kissing my labia as his tongue lashes out against my sensitive clit. Lifting and guiding me through the whole process.

To be his is to feel the epitome of vulnerability and security all at once. This big, broad-shouldered brute hunches down, licking at my freshly cleaned slit, his muscles rippling as he pushes my thighs apart. The swirl of his tongue around my tiny clit so torturously skillful.

My back arches and for a second I think I'm going to twitch and hurt him, but then I remember it's Mikhail. I can't hurt him. It's like he reads my thoughts, because he grips my thighs harder, making sure I know that he's the one in control, even as he pampers me with his mouth.

"Oh god," I gasp, clutching the blankets as my entire body grows warmer. I lose all my thoughts, all my hesitations, all my insecurities as he lavishes me with attention.

There he is, this older man, made of muscle and determination, carrying the scars of a harsh life, using all his power to hold me down and please me. To keep me in place as he takes his time, taking a taste of me. And the way he does it never made it seem for one moment like it's anything but his desire to drink me in and have every bit of me that pushed him to do this.

Mikhail has to have me. All of me. All to himself. But not like some rich man hoards his gold, no. It isn't just enough to have me, he has to experience every facet of me. Savor me. And that's what it looks like as I watch him eat me out, his head moving, a low, guttural growl rumbling from out of his broad chest to hum through his lips and he tongues against my slit.

Even though I can't help but squirm, I'm overcome by the sensuality and the soft pleasure he's bestowing on me. I lick my lips, but I'm panting so fast that they're immediately dry again.

"Oh Mikhail," I moan, my fingers going to his head,

entwining in his thick hair as my other hand grips the comforter. "Just like that!"

But he does it as his own pace, torturing me, teasing me along the brink a while until I'm a panting, squirming mess. Only when he's satisfied with having his fill does he help push me over that ledge I've been teetering on, his tongue masterfully swirling around my clit until I'm crying out and gushing with pleasure.

My world goes dark as I feel blind a moment, slumping back onto the bed breathlessly. When I slowly come back to reality, it's with my dark, rugged lover over me. My ankles are in his hands as he keeps me splayed wide, his dick teasing along my glistening pussy.

"I meant every word I said," he growls, nudging the thick, purple crown of his manhood against my woman-hood. He speaks as he sinks down into me, spearing me on his manhood as his dark voice rumbles with pleasure, "I am going to knock you up and make you my woman for life, *kotika*."

"I know," I manage, but my head is still spinning, and I'd say anything to get him back inside of me. I want his warmth, his touch, inside and out. But it's not for me to say. He has all the power, all the control, and no matter how much I nudge my hips towards him, I know he won't take me until he can't stand the temptation any more.

I watch his manhood pulse as I tease, smearing my glistening honey along his cock as he stares at me with such intensity. Is it love? Lust? Both, I know instinctually. The smolder in his dark gaze is communicating with me on a sub-human level, even though he's never said the words.

He sweeps down slowly and presses his lips to mine,

taking my mouth with a deep, passionate kiss. Only then does he push in, spearing me once more, stretching me around his manhood and making me moan all over again, as if it were the very first time. From there, it's the slow, steady pump of his hips as he claims me anew.

I'm fresh and clean, but he's making me feel filthy in all the right ways. He's torturing me with pleasure, and it's only when I'm screaming and the bed is torn apart by my frantic grasping that he seems to be letting up at all. I feel like I can't take it anymore, my throbbing clit pressed against his loins, my ankles wrapped around his neck, but he doesn't relent.

My paler skin meets his hard flesh, his short tangle of dark hair above his shaft tickling my sensitive nub as he pumps into me. It's torturous! And with how big he is, the strain he puts on my narrow little slit is almost too much to bear, but he draws the moment out, taking *his* time with me. Slow and sweet.

I've been flailing and bunching up blankets around me for some time when I first start screaming out, "I can't take it!" But he's still not done with me, even as I feel his dick swell. He's ravenous, like a mighty warrior savoring his gladiatorial rewards, and he won't stop until he's done.

As I feel him near, he reaches out, taking hold of my face, pointing me right towards him as he stares into my eyes so intensely.

"I am going to breed you, my pet," he husks, his gaze not letting mine wander. "I am going to keep you with me and make you swell with my child. And when you give birth, I'll plant another seed in your belly...and another..." His gaze grows darker, more intense and I feel him throbbing inside me painfully wide, my poor pink little labia stretched raw and reddish from his long use of me.

Some part of me screams that I shouldn't let a killer come in me—again—but I shove that voice down, because what he's saying...

I want that. I want exactly that.

"Yes!" I cry out, "Please, I need it."

I'm on the cusp of another orgasm, but I do my best to keep it down and watch. Watch the glorious sight of this ripped god pump his dick into me a few final times. See the way his veiny trunk of a cock splits me open, glistening with my honey, until at last, he buries it inside me one final time.

I watch as he tenses, and sinewy muscle bulges across his broad shoulders, over his biceps and down his rocky stomach. Then I witness the glorious sight of this massive brute pump, short little coital pumps, and I'm able to feel him piercing too deep inside, unleashing all that virile seed as far inside me as it'll go.

And I do it all knowing that each new spurt of his cream was another enhanced guarantee I'd bear this murderer's child.

That's the thought that does it, and I can't hold back anymore. I let loose a scream of pleasure that surpasses all the others and I sink my nails into his bulging forearms, quaking so intensely as I climax upon his dick again, a flood of my slick honey coating his manhood, flooding down around his heavy balls.

When finally we come down from our mutual high, panting for breath and glistening with perspiration, I can't help but giggle a bit.

"I'm going to need another shower now that you dirtied me all up again," I tease.

He gives a wry smile and kisses me sweetly, grabbing up the towel from the floor and using it to cup our loins as he pulls from me, keeping our blissful mess from spilling out. That tender little act is just one among many, but it touches me deeply as he pulls me into him with his arm, holding me to his chest as he tugs the blankets up around us.

"Worry about showers later, *kotika*," he says gruffly, turning off the bedside light. "For now, you and me need to rest," he says.

I know he's right, and after... how many orgasms? I'm exhausted. All the pain of earlier, the aches in my wrists and leg return, though they're duller now, numbed by our mutual pleasure.

"That was amazing," I purr as I curl into his chest, my fingers lazily stroking the bed of hair there.

"You were amazing, little *kotika*," he says in a deep gruff.

"What does that mean?" I ask, my voice faltering as hoarseness takes over. "*Kotika?*"

"Kitty cat," he explains patiently. "You are my little *kotika*," he says, and though it's dark now, I can feel his smile.

My heart's still pumping even as he idly strokes my hair, and I wonder if I'll ever calm down enough to get to sleep. But it doesn't take us long before we're both out, the exhausting day claiming us both in a deep sleep.

When I wake up, it has to be a whole new day, because I feel like I've slept for an eternity, but the orange glow of evening sunset spills into the room. We must've slept for nearly a full twenty four hours!

But that's not the truly alarming thing—what strikes me is the sight of Mikhail sat on the edge of the bed, phone to his ear.

"What's wrong?" I ask, but he holds up a hand to silence me.

"Get dressed," he says tersely, and I see the seriousness in his eyes. "Now."

CHAPTER 19

MIKHAIL

Nikki's voice still rings in my ears.

"Gregor knows everything. He knows you hid the girl, that you killed Vasili…I've never seen him so angry, Mikhail. And the way he looked at me? He's gonna be gunning for everyone you've ever cared for, if that's what it takes to get to you," she'd said.

I'd told her to go into hiding, given her the address for my old safehouse in New York, the one I'd taken Alicia to originally, in case she can't get any further in time. But nobody is safe anymore. Not with me around.

"What's wrong?" Alicia asks me, pulling me out of my own head as we get ready, and I head to the closet, pulling out a shirt, pants, and jacket. She's listening to me now, getting dressed, and I know she must realize how serious this is. She's fought me on everything else so far, but now she's being obedient. It somehow hurts to see that, and know it's my fault.

"Somehow, Gregorovich knows I spared you, kept you

safe, and killed Vasili," I say as evenly as I can, but we have to go.

"Who's Gregorovich?"

"One of the biggest bosses in New York."

"Wait… was that the other Russian guy Vasili was talking to on the phone while he was torturing me?" she asks, fear quaking her voice.

Shit. So that was it.

"I guess that's how he overheard it all when you came to rescue me," she says, and she's right.

"Rookie mistake," I growl at myself. But my head had been fuzzy. It was a miracle that I pulled off the rescue at all with all the blood I'd lost by then.

"Aren't we safe here?" she asks me as she pulls on her clothes. Unfortunately, I have no extra women's things, so I do my best to offer her one of my oversized shirts to replace her bloodstained top.

"No," I say firmly.

"But… you said it's secure," she says, clearly not grasping the severity of the situation. And how could she? I took her out of her simple life, where her biggest concerns were getting recognized at her job. She wasn't made for my life, for the things I have to do.

I grasp her by the shoulders, holding her tight as I gaze down into her eyes.

"This isn't a thug like Vasili. Gregorovich is a boss. He commands an army with the backing of a fortune. He's less a criminal than a warlord. None of the usual rules apply anymore, Allie. None of them. He will find us here if we stay long enough, he'll find us anywhere we go. Hiding is no longer an option. Running only works for so long," I say, impressing upon her the seriousness of this situation.

But I see the wide-eyed fear and depression setting into her gaze.

"Then…then what? We just…give up?" she asks, her lower lip trembling, making me want to kiss and suckle it. Damn it, I can't get distracted. Not now. I want to soothe and comfort her, but there's only one way I know to do that.

"No," I say firmly, lightening my grip on her. "I am going to take you back to the gang and arrange a meeting with the over bosses. If Gregorovich is going to wage war, I am going to call in the big guns," I tell her firmly, knowing it's the only course of action.

But her brow furrows, she disapproves immediately.

"But… you can't take me to the gang again," she objects as I take out a burner phone, a disposable thing I'll use but once before discarding it. "Mikhail," she says grabbing my bicep as I dial up a number I've not ever had to call.

I block her out as the call goes through, and a dark voice picks up on the other end.

"Yes?" a man's voice says on the other side.

"I need to arrange a meeting," I say, grim and simple.

"When?" he asks, knowing well that I would never call unless it was serious. Direly serious.

"Immediately," I tell him and he goes quiet a moment, as Alicia tugs at my arm again.

"Mikhail!" she cries, looking panicked. So I put my arm around her and hold her close.

"You know the place. Tonight," he says, and that's it. The call is over.

"You can't just dump me off with them! Not after what happened last time! I'm no safer with them than I am with you!" she pleads frantically.

"Get ready," I stress as I finish up pulling on my jacket and then open a back panel behind the clothes in the closet. There I store some guns, ammo, a knife, and other equipment, everything I'd need to take out a small army.

She takes a step back, and I can feel the fear that jolts through her. She's been with me so long, it feels like, but she's still surprised by the ugliness I hide. A second later, though, and she's back at my side, the momentary shock evaporated.

"Holy shit," she curses, and the dirtiness of her words distracts me again, just for a second. I'm not at my best with her at my side, that's really why I don't want her there. Protecting her means putting a bit of distance between us so I don't get fouled up when I need to work.

When I need to kill.

Strapping some guns and knives to my body, I'm wearing a heavier leather jacket to better mask their presence. I give her a small knife, strap it to her calf, and add two small guns, giving a quick rundown of how to use them. Then I guide her to the door, grabbing up some food from the cupboards along the way. It's all non-perishable stuff, but some protein bars and bottles of water from the fridge will have to do. I've not eaten in so long, and I'm still getting over the injuries I suffered, so nourishment will be needed.

I take her on out of the building, down towards the basement garage. I open the door and very nearly guide her out first before my instincts kick in, and I hold her back.

Not a moment too soon, because a shotgun blast rings out, enough to mow down anyone that'd be standing there and leave only a bloody pulp.

"Get back!" I say, pushing her to the wall out of the way. The doors on the other side now, I can't reach across to close it.

I hold back and wait, but there's not much more to do. I could take Alicia to the other exit, but there's a good chance if they found this hideaway, they've staked out that exit too and are just as ready there.

Their impatience pays off for us, though, when one of the men comes to the door. I grab his wrists, hit him in the face, and step out into the doorway, using his body as a shield. Another shotgun blast fills the building, but the meaty thug in front of me absorbs the blow with a pained, dying groan.

I raise my gun over the dying man's shoulder and fire. One shot is all I need again, and the shooter is down, never to get up.

I toss the corpse in my arms into the garage, and another man shoots for it, his itchy trigger finger anxious and aiming for the first sign of movement. These men were sent here to kill me, not capture. Gregor isn't playing games.

But that one moment of distraction is all I need, and I slip out, shooting down the man that just plugged the corpse of his comrade. He fires off a shot as he sprawls back against the wall, short one eye. But that bullet of his goes astray.

"C'mon," I say, grabbing hold of Alicia with one hand as I take us out to make way for a car.

I'm hoping luck is with us, and there I see it: another

thug waiting by the stolen car we got here in, and I realize that there must've been something in Vasili's vehicle used to track us down. Of course. Another amateur mistake, but one I couldn't have avoided in my condition at the time. I'll blame myself later.

Instead, I take fire at the goon, able to take him out before he can pop off a shot at all. Alicia starts to rush towards the car but I stop her.

"No, we're not taking that one," I say, but she furrows her brow and looks around at the empty parking garage.

"Then what?" she asks, sleek black gun in hand.

I take her by the hand and guide her around a brick wall into a hidden nook. It's so simple, but so hard to see. The human mind is easily tricked by such optical illusions. There, waiting for us, is a plain black car that I keep at the safe house in case of need. Just another little precautionary method. And a relatively cheap one, as far as they come in my line of work.

"Get in," I tell her, and she rushes around to the passenger side.

As I move to get into the driver's seat a gunshot rings out, and I freeze.

I missed something. Someone. They got the drop on me.

I look up and see Alicia's face, the world moving as if in slow motion. Her expression is one of horror. Fright.

I can feel my heartbeat. The mistakes are catching up with me. I'd let myself be led astray by feelings, and it's cost me. Not just my first mistake of over a decade, not my second, my third. Now… this?

But as she lowers her gun, I hear the sound of a heavy

set man's body hit the pavement and realize—it's not mine.

I turn around and see that from out of the shadows, the killer behind me slumped down dead. Or nearly so. Her aim was far from perfect, and that chest wound wasn't guaranteed to do him in. I finish the job for her, and hope it clears her conscience.

"You saved us," I tell her in soft praise. "Now get in!" There's no more time to waste.

So much has happened. And the beautiful young woman I rescued from death has faced more than any woman should ever have to. I start up the car and we tear out into the garage. It's not until we're about to exit onto the street that another goon pops his head out, and I blow it off of him from out my window. The guy coming up behind him is victim to my fender. Probably not dead, but when he hits the pavement, he won't be up in time.

We're moving on down the road, and I realize...

She's right. She's no safer with Leon, not now. Leon's dealing with his own shit, and I know there's going to be guns there, too. Besides, if she's going to be sticking with me, then I'm going to have to get used to her butting her cute nose into my business.

"New plan," I say firmly, trying to steady my mind. To bring that killer instinct to full focus again, checking all points around me, making sure we're not being followed.

There's no more room for mistakes, not from me, not for her. Together, we're going to have to prove ourselves stronger than Gregorovich and his army. If she and I have any hope at a future, then this will have to be how it is, and we're going to have to be better than I was when I was alone.

My head needs to be clear, but it's filled with lust and desire for her. It's not how I'm used to working, but I can take my love and I can make it into a deadly weapon, just as I took my loneliness and hurt and turned it into one. I can make this anger and rage and desire to protect even more potent than what I had before.

These emotions don't have to weaken me. They can be a source of my strength, and once I tap into them, I know we'll be unstoppable.

"You're with me, *kotika*," I tell her. "To the end."

CHAPTER 20

ALICIA

We're driving down the road, making our way out of town, and my head is abuzz with thought.

I just shot a man.

The gun is still cradled in my hand, upon my lap. And I'd used it to shoot a man dead. I'd never even held a gun in all my years before Mikhail. The closest I'd come was playing light-gun games at the arcade with an ex-boyfriend!

Part of me feels like I should roll down my window and fling the gun away. Part of my feels like I should clutch it and never let go. Overall, I'm mostly surprised by how well I'm handling it.

"I shot a man dead," I mutter aloud without realizing it.

"Not quite dead," Mikhail says, keeping his eyes upon the road. "I took care of that for you. But you saved both our lives, Allie. That's what matters."

And despite the moral qualms of it all, I feel he's right. Just like I've felt he's been right about so much.

"Here," he says, taking one hand off the wheel and fishing out a phone from his jacket. "Call your mother's place. Tell the care worker to get your mom out of there, take her to safety. Some friend's place, anywhere that will keep her safe for a bit longer," he explains. And I realize he's been true to his word about looking out for my mom.

I was right to trust him.

I know instantly that Mikhail was having someone check on her this whole time, just as he promised. Just as he told me he would. I felt like a rotten daughter for not checking in before now, but being on the run...there just hasn't been time. To know that even through all this, he has been thinking of her, even when I got wrapped up in my own head...

Maybe that's why I can't stop the word 'love' from running through my brain.

Every time I try to tell myself that he's just a killer, he proves me wrong. He's something—someone—so much more. He might kill, but no one who's innocent.

He protected me from whatever my asshole boss had planned, saved me from an even worse torture at the hands of Vasili, and now I know he was looking out for my family, too.

I quickly call my mom, each ring feeling like eternity.

Please pick up, I plead with her silently. *Please, Mom, I need to hear your voice.*

If something has happened to her, I'll never forgive myself...

Her old style answering machine kicks in, some relic from the 90s that still has a novelty recording. My mom couldn't stand to replace it, not with the sound of her and my deceased father's voice sing-songing their way through the greeting. It makes me tear up.

"Mom, pick up," I say, hoping she's nearby. "Mom, are you there?"

Seconds pass, and I start to lose hope, giving Mikhail and uncertain look, and he squeezes my thigh in a comforting manner. And then I hear a click on the other end of the connection.

"Mom?"

A laughing man's voice answers, though. "Hello? She'll be right with you!"

Who the hell is this? Is what I want to ask. But instead, I wait for my mom. It's only a few seconds later that her giggling voice answers. I don't know if I've ever heard her giggle before.

"Alicia? Honey! It's so good to hear from you. Sorry about that, Hernando and I were salsa dancing in the kitchen!"

What has been going on since this happened and who is Hernando?

"Mom, all that is going to have to wait. For now, I need you to pack and go to a nice hotel somewhere, alright? On the Upper East Side, somewhere ritzy. I'm going to dip into my savings to treat you to a nice weekend! And you can bring... Hernando?"

"Her care worker," Mikhail says to me softly.

Oh. Well then.

"Oh honey, that's too much! And Hernando and I are fine right here. When are you coming home? I'm planning on making a Sunday meal this week."

"Soon, Mom," I say, my throat clamping up. "Just go out, enjoy the weekend. Can I talk to Hernando?"

"Fine, fine, but I have my appointment this week, remember."

"Yea, Mom. I remember." Since when did she remember that though?

A second later, and Hernando takes the phone from my mom and I glance at Mikhail, silently wondering how much Hernando knows about him. Probably not much.

"Hey Hernando, Mom's going to fight me on this, but I'm going to give her a nice weekend in a ritzy hotel on the Upper East Side, okay? I want you to go with her and take care of her. Here's my credit card info for the booking," I say, quickly wrapping up the call. At least Hernando knows how to take orders.

And then I sit back, the phone call ringing in my head.

"She hasn't sounded that happy since Dad died," I say quietly. "She's never let anyone else take care of her, only me..."

"Don't worry," Mikhail says, perhaps mistaking my words for worry, "Hernando is the best in his business. He can be trusted. I made sure of that before I hired him." The stern look on his broad-jawed face tells me exactly how serious he took my mother's care.

It takes a little longer for it to dawn on me that this is likely the nicest thing that anyone has ever done for me. I could excuse his saving me for some twisted moral code, or because he has the hots for me. But taking care of my mom—something he did since he first took me captive, apparently—is something altogether different.

It shows that from that first day together, he never lied to me. He never deceived me.

He has been the man he told me he was, and for better or worse, I know that we're in this together now. I reach out, touching the back of his hand, letting him feel the slight weight of my skin on his.

"Thank you, Mikhail," I say, and I hope he can hear the earnestness in my tone.

He doesn't respond immediately, just gives the slightest crook of a smile before twisting his one hand around and holding mine as he drives us along into the darkening night. We hold hands like that in quiet for a while as we drive through forested back roads away from the cities and people.

It's the kind of scene that should send chills down a girl's spine: driving into a dark, forested road, away from all witnesses, in the clutches of a killer.

But after all that's happened, my trust in him rewarded, my own abilities to defend myself—and him—proven, I feel so very calm. In control. For the first time in my life, I feel like I can trust my own judgment. My own abilities.

Mikhail pulls us off the road into an old sports field, which looks out of use.

"What are we doing here?" I ask, not quite putting all the pieces together. There's no buildings as such, unless you count an outhouse and what looks to be a padlocked storage shed.

"We have some time to kill," he says, opening his door and getting out. "Come with me."

He shoots me a wry grin before getting out, and I follow. I'm still holding the gun in my lap as I climb out. It's dark and I can't see well, the white paint on the structures the only thing making them stand out.

The stars glow above us, just a sliver of the moon that barely lights our way as the silence of the rural area stretches out. It's so quiet, it almost hurts after living in New York for so long. All there is around us is crickets and a bird in the distance.

Mikhail leaves my side and goes over to the storage shed, hitting a switch along the side and making lights go up around the grassy area.

For a second, I'm blinded, having to shield my eyes from the sudden light, but then I can see what I'm looking at. An abandoned baseball field, the grass grown out a bit, but still cleared enough that there doesn't seem to be any mosquitos, the breeze keeping them at bay. A few yards away is a row of bleachers, and beyond that, simply trees.

It's actually beautiful, for an old sports field.

Mikhail just walks towards me, my giant, mafia brute looking dashing in his shirt and jacket, while I feel a little silly in a mix of his clothes and mine.

"Take out your gun," he says to me, and I do after a moment's delay.

"You did very well today. Saved both our lives," he says, resting his large hand upon my shoulder, squeezing before he guides me into the field. "But without training, it's a miracle you hit anything. Especially under pressure. If we're going to survive all of this, you'll need more than your wits about you."

He crouches a little behind me, his thick arms wrapped about, guiding my own slender limbs up, positioning me according to his exacting expectations.

"When you hold a gun, you have to do so like this. It's the best way to absorb shock and make sure your aim is true," he explains to me in that deep, husky voice of his, every word a tickle upon my eardrum.

He feels so warm and reassuring, but I understand why he wants to teach me. Because maybe he won't always be right there to reassure me or finish the job. I'm going to need to learn to stand on my own two feet and rely on my guts and wits if I'm going to be living in his world.

If we're to survive this night, then I need to make sure I'm ready.

I take a breath in and nod. "Where do I point?"

"See the fence at the other end of the field?" he asks, and I nod. "Aim for the white picket between the two broken ones."

He helps me keep my stance as I aim, his breathing growing so shallow I can barely detect it anymore.

"Now, before you take a shot, you inhale... hold your breath. Don't let your breathing interfere with your aim, or else you will miss every time," he explains, and I nod, doing as he instructed and holding my breath.

"Now shoot."

As the gun's bang resounds around us, I notice I missed.

"In a fight, you won't have time to check and see if you made a shot, and I don't have time to teach you so you have trust in your aim. This time, I want you to take your shot and quickly pop off another round. Then another. Making sure to realign your shot each time. The kickback will ruin your aim each time you shoot, remember. Now go," he says.

It sounds like a lot to remember, but I do my best. I inhale, letting my shoulders relax a little so that I can get a better grip. I'm scared, the loud sounds startling me each time, but it feels powerful as well. The thought that this could save my life—or Mikhail's—is what keeps me centered.

And then I squeeze the trigger. I don't even bother to wait this time, though. Instead, I keep staring ahead, my breath burning in my lungs as I pull it again. And again.

As I release my breath, he squeezes my shoulders reassuringly.

"Good, but don't hold your breath for so long next time. Work on timing it better. You need oxygen in a fight to stay alert, hold your breath only as long as you need to. Now try it again," he says, and we repeat the exercise a few times until I'm able to hit the target reliably at least once. That requires him retreating to his car to grab a couple extra clips, but he displays such impressive patience with me the whole time.

"I'm gettin' good, right?" I say, smiling up at him as I twist at the waist. He nods right back.

"You're a natural. But don't get too confident. Standing there in a peaceful field and taking your time with shots is nothing like a fight. I know you can keep your cool in a crisis though, so now you're going to practice shooting and moving. Your aim is always better up closer, and you never want to stand in one spot too long. It makes you an easy target to others. Watch me," he says, and he pulls out his own gun.

In an impressive display I can never hope to imitate, he holds his handgun out with one hand—not two, like me— and advances on the target. His even pace takes him closer with each of three shots, and I can't help but marvel at how each of his bullets strikes its mark. It makes my record seem trivial.

"Try it," he encourages me, and my first attempt is a

disaster. I miss all three shots again, just like starting over. And I must look a little crestfallen, because Mikhail squeezes my shoulder as he guides me back to my starting position.

"Moving and shooting is rough, don't let it dissuade you," he says in that deep, calming voice of his. "If you can manage to hit the target at all, you're better than most. Now try again, and remember what I said about your breathing? Try to take your shots on those brief moments your two feet are planted and you're still. It's all about timing."

It's complicated, but I'm determined, and so I repeat the motions, trying to recreate the magic of watching him move. He's a trained professional and has been doing this for...how long, exactly? I can't expect to be as good as him in a single night, but his confidence in me is what spurs me on. If he's an expert, and he has faith in me, then I should have faith in myself too.

Besides, I did take down the guy who was going to kill us both. I did what I had to, when push came to shove, and if I could only just trust my instincts once more...

We repeat the maneuvers again and again and again, until finally, eventually... I do it. And I literally jump for joy, wearing a grin two sizes too big for my face.

"I did it!" I squeal, and he's grinning proudly at me, looking on with a look that's half fatherly pride, half manly appreciation.

"Good work," he says, swooping in and kissing me as his arm sweeps around my torso. His tongue pries past my lips as we make out in the middle of the field, until at last we break away, and I peer into his dark eyes.

"How long have you been doing this, Mikhail?" I ask a

little breathlessly, my heart thumping inside my chest so hard I swear it's about to break free.

His expression loses some of its soft warmth and goes back to its harsher, set-in-stone look.

"Shooting? Since I was a boy, when my father taught me to handle an old service rifle," he explains to me, ever patient with me, even if he is the merciless angel of death to others. "If you mean life as a criminal, longer still."

He hands me a clip and teaches me how to unload and load the gun.

"Did you have a hard life then?" I ask, even if part of me says it's probably not a thing to talk about.

"My father was a criminal piece of shit from the day I was born. He only looked after me because of the benefits from the state it earned him. And then when the old government fell, he kept me around to help him rob homes, stores, and even graves," he says, an obvious lack of love for his father in his words.

"You robbed graves?" I say, my nose crinkling at the thought. As if that's the worst thing I know him to have done.

"*Da*," he says, then instructs me to try my shooting again.

"They were ugly times. Honest working people found themselves struggling to survive for the first time in generations," he explains to me before getting me to go through the practice routine once more. "But my father was made for such times. He had never lasted a full day in a factory or office. He knew how to make a living from chaos and despair."

I frown a little at that thought. Making a living from chaos and despair?

"So he's what got you into organized crime?" I ask.

"Not entirely. Now again," he says, and I shoot once more, three more shots as I advance on the target. "I left home to get away from my father as soon as I could. Joined the army. Fought Chechens in a bombed out hole that was once their home. Saw war and ugliness that even my father couldn't fathom," he says, and I can see the darkness in his eyes, like tunnels into his soul gouged out by a hard life of pain. Received and given.

It all kind of falls into place. I understand, now, how he can do what he does. Why he must. I lived a pretty cushy life, all told. Sure, I struggled and felt loss. I mourned for a long time when Dad died, and then I had to start caring for Mom, and I know I've complained about that to anyone who'd listen. My studies in college to become a doctor, or at least a pharmacist or chemist, were hampered by my need to look after my mom and pay the bills.

But his life is like something I couldn't even consider, and I have a newfound respect for how he did what he had to. He's been so cold and hard throughout his entire life, betrayed by the people who were supposed to have his back.

And then I waltzed into his life; maybe that can help him?

Maybe, after all this settles down, and if we survive the next few days, I could really be a person that he can come to count on and respect.

BANG! BANG! BANG!

And I did it. I managed to hit the target twice as I advanced on it, leaving the long fence with a few less picket tips.

"I-" but before I can declare my victory, he claims me in

an embrace again, holding me in his arms, kissing me. He takes his time, his strong hands rubbing at my shoulders and spine until finally I melt. And only then does he relent.

"When this is done, and your life is safe from Gregorovich," he says, peering into my eyes with those two dark tunnels into his soul, "I will marry you. And we will live in a beautiful home, with the sound of many little feet running about us. And your mother will stay in a guest suite. I will make a life with you, like I had no inkling of knowing I needed all these years."

I can feel a sob threatening me, happy tears springing to my eyes before I blink them away. I didn't even know I wanted a life like that, a life with a killer, a life with him.

But when he says it, I know it's all I've ever wanted and never knew I did. Someone I can be totally honest with, someone who can share in all the pain and joy of life and never abandon me. Someone who can protect me and love me, no matter what happens.

And if we could survive the last couple weeks together, we can survive anything that comes our way.

His mouth presses in against mine, tender and soft, filled with such affection, and my tongue meets his in kind.

When he breaks the kiss again, his words coming out gravelly and low, I'm stunned by what he has to say.

"Man of power or simple means, I love you, will love you for all time, and I will protect you, Alicia."

There's no way I can hold back the tears now, so I quickly swipe under my eyes as my lips tremble. I can't believe what I'm hearing.

This murderer is in love with me.

"I'm in love with you, too," I say back, before I can even think about it.

His chiseled face breaks with a genuine smile, unlike any I'd ever seen him bear. But the touching moment is all too short, as the sound of crunching gravel and the lights of an approaching vehicle light up the unpaved back road, and I raise my gun with a newly blossomed instinct for survival.

I'm not going to fall in love moments before death.

CHAPTER 21

MIKHAIL

I hear the approaching car a moment later than I should have, as evidenced by the fact that my girl jumped to attention first, despite my lifetime of study. She's a natural at this, I guess, but when I look, I immediately see the vehicle make and know who it must be.

"It's okay," I tell Alicia, putting my hand on her arm and guiding her aim away from the approaching vehicle. "It's an old friend."

The car comes to a halt and it shuts off, leaving just the dark silhouette inside.

Though I cautioned Alicia, I keep my own hand near to my gun. Petyr is an old friend alright, but old friends can become new enemies. And anyone can be tailed. Especially now, when tensions are running high. Who knows who could've gotten to him, and what other enemies I've made.

"Mikhail," comes the familiar voice as he steps out of his car, and I give Alicia a nudge to stand back as I step forward.

"Petyr," I say as we move to meet in quiet inspection of each other. He's put on some weight.

"Comrade!" Petyr exclaims, and I can feel some of the tension lift as we embrace.

"You've lost none of your strength!" I say in English for Alicia's sake, and it's true. Bigger he might be, but beneath that layer of added padding, he's as strong as a bear.

"You've lost nothing, I can see," Petyr says as he pulls back in his thick, expensive suit and overcoat. Too warm for the time of year.

"Only gained enemies," I reply, and Petyr nods in return.

"Is always the way for men like us, *nyet*?" he says, casting nary a glance in Alicia's direction. He's all business as usual. "What is the problem you drag me out here for in the evening, Mikhail? You could have been boss of your own territory, need turn to nobody."

"That is the problem. I turned down the offer when I shouldn't have. And Gregorovich has made a mess of things," I say.

"That sounds very serious," Petyr says, glancing in Alicia's direction for the first time. "Does this have something to do with your lady?" he asks in Russian, but I answer in English.

"In part, it does. As you know, Gregor had that hit against the Chechens and that congressman, and all has spiraled out of control. He sicced Vasili on me and my girl to cover the tracks, as if I can't be trusted," I tell him, a bit of a bending of the truth, but not an outright lie.

But Petyr looks confused.

"Wait," he says, hands up, "a hit against the congressman? What- you mean… you and Gregor did that?" he asks, sounding increasingly agitated as time passes. He curses in our mother tongue. "Mikhail, do you have any idea what you fucked up? Those were no Chechens! Those were our men! That massacre fucked up our business royally!"

Now it's my turn to be confused, my brow furrowing.

"Gregor said the hit was sanctioned by you and the Bratva," I say, and for a moment I can tell Petyr is studying me. Trying to find out if I'm lying. Even old friendships face their tests in this business.

"Mikhail," he says in a low, tempered voice, "we were comrades in arms through war. New York City would be yours for the taking if you only asked. Are you playing games with me now?"

"*Nyet!*" I say, falling back into Russian, leaving Alicia out of the loop as I speak, "I passed that chance up, and did Gregor's orders as was my place. That is the only mistake I have made!" I say, but it wasn't quite the only mistake. Just the biggest.

I can feel Alicia behind me, shifting her weight from foot to foot restlessly. She can feel the tension, even if she doesn't understand our tongue.

"Brother, this is serious, if Gregor has done this he is attempting to make a move on the whole bratva," Petyr says. But then my attention is drawn away by the sound of a crack, like someone stepping on a branch. Petyr hears it too, because the two of us grab for our guns and dive at about the same time. Only I dive for Alicia to throw her to the ground. Except she's one step ahead of us two old war buddies even, popping off a shot just before I fling us to the ground.

The thunderous sound of guns firing, bullets whizzing past us as we hit the dirt just in the nick of time.

To her credit, Alicia doesn't scream, and she moves her gun away from my gut so it doesn't accidentally go off. Her mind is quick, even in the thick of it, but all three of us are at a disadvantage. The lights are behind us, and the gunfire is in the trees. The only shelter is the shed a few yards away and the car. I don't have to tell her or Petyr—we all start shimmying towards our cover in near unison.

Petyr hides behind his car as we make for the shed, there are some close calls, and I feel a pinch in my calf as a bullet grazes me. But there's no time to see the damage. I rise up as we get behind the shed and my leg holds, so it's good enough. I pull the switch, shutting off the lights so that we're all at an equal sight advantage.

"Keep a low profile, harder to hit you that way," I mutter to Alicia as the gunfire becomes more sporadic now that the men after us have been deprived of the light advantage. "Stay here and pop off a few shots to give me cover. But never fire from the same exact spot twice," I caution her before slipping around the corner behind us to come out the other side of the shed.

"Wait, Mik-" Alicia starts, but cuts off, doing her duty like a real soldier, after only just one training session.

She fires that first shot, and it does the trick—the gunmen shoot in her direction but she's a clever girl who waits behind cover. And I've never been so damn proud in all my life. Not of any medal or accomplishment I ever earned, that's for certain.

With the shots focused on her and Petyr, I slip under cover of darkness into the tree line. There I'm at my best. Under cover of night, brush and tree, I'm a wraith. I know how to move through such terrain without making a sound, and I creep up on our attackers, their muzzle flashes a dead giveaway as I get nearer.

I reach down, taking my hunting knife out of its sheath, because tonight, I'm going to hunt the deadliest of prey.

Ducking low, knife in one hand, gun in the other, I come up on the first man. It won't be as smooth and calculated as my hit on the hotel that night I met Alicia; things are moving too fast for that, her life on the line with every moment more we spend here. But I spring forward, knife lancing into the back of one gunman, driving right between his ribs and into his heart as I lift my gun over his shoulder and blow the head off another thug.

There's a third man here, and he turns towards me, firing a shot. But the man dying in my arms serves as a shield of sorts and buys me time to kill him too. That's three down, but I know there's at least one more.

I hear the sound of Petyr crying out in pain as he's hit, and I dash for his car in the dark. Bullets whizz by me but miss.

"You okay?" I ask Petyr, but before he can answer, a man with a submachine gun comes out of the bushes, blazing away at us. I crouch behind the car as the bullets shred its metal doors. I roll along the ground and pop up over the trunk of the car, blowing the man's head off before he can turn his gun towards me.

Everything goes silent as I duck back down and take a breath.

"You alive, comrade?" I ask my old friend, and there's only silence. I move back beside him and I find out why. He's busy tying some torn piece of his expensive suit around his arm with his mouth, to prevent the blood from draining out of his wounded limb. I'm relieved, I'll admit. Few buddies of mine have survived this long.

"Good work," I tell him, but all relief drains away as the most distressing sound ever rises up behind us.

"Mikhail!" Alicia's voice rises in panic.

CHAPTER 22

ALICIA

What am I doing?

I'm in a gunfight at an old baseball field in the middle of nowhere. Just months ago, I was a college student, wanting to earn enough to look out for my mom's care.

What scares me most is how I'm keeping it together. For so long, I watched Mikhail and wondered how he could do it. How he could shoot and kill others. And here I am, doing just that without hesitation. When it came down to it—them or me—I chose me without blinking.

I can't see things clearly, but the cries of pain and then the two distinctive sounds of Mikhail's gun firing let me know he's claimed some lives in our defense. And then I see him dart from the edge of the forest to his friend's car like a ghost in the night.

I might be able to keep my cool surprisingly well in a fight, but I can't move like he does or do the things he does with such precision and expertise.

Not yet, a voice in my head says, and that puts a chill down my spine.

Is that where my life is going? Training to become a killer with Mikhail?

I push aside those thoughts. They're trivial. It's too soon to relax. That much is abundantly clear as I watch a man walk out of the bushes, gun blazing. I line up a shot, but Mikhail takes him down first. *He's so damn good.*

But as he and his friend Petyr settle down again, I keep an eye out. And then I see it.

We're not done.

"Mikhail!" I cry out, but even he can't be quick enough to save his own ass this time. The angle is all wrong, the gunman is too close.

I'm all there is between my lover and death.

I hold my breath and fire.

BANG!

I step forward and as my feet touch the ground again…

BANG!

One more step forward and… BANG!

I keep pulling the trigger as the man topples over. He's a bullet-riddled mess as he hits the ground. And I'm still pulling the trigger, even as my clip empties.

He's dead.

Mikhail pounces up, puts his arms around me and pulls me behind cover of the car in case any more are out there.

"You did it," he says to me in a husky breath, so full of pride. "You saved all our asses."

"You owe me a cheesecake later," I quip, looking between the two of them. "For now, I don't really wanna hang around here."

I'm out of breath, but Mikhail's strong arms comfort me, soothe away the agitation in my shoulders. It was a rush to save them, to do what I had to, and my entire body feels like this intense tingly sensation. It doesn't feel right.

It kinda feels like I'm horny, which definitely isn't appropriate right now. Is that what they talk about when they say your adrenaline spikes during a fight?

"You have to go end Gregor, Mikhail," Petyr says as he finishes binding up his wound, and Mikhail checks his own leg, finding little more than a superficial graze.

We hear a groan from nearby, and Mikhail and I are immediately on alert. But it quickly becomes clear that it's the sound of a dying man.

Approaching the spot with care, Mikhail finds him, and I realize, judging by the spot he was in, it had to be the guy I shot at the very beginning. I did it.

He's nursing a wound in his gut, his blood looking like black oil over his hands, not at all what I'd expect. I find myself grossly fascinated, which is a far cry from who I was—who I thought I was—just a couple weeks ago.

"Tell me what you know," Mikhail says darkly. But the wounded man just pants. Mikhail bends down and stabs that knife of his into the man's hand, making him cry out.

"H-he has a girl! Held captive! In case you get away!" He says, his agony palpable.

"What girl?" Mikhail asks as Petyr moves off to check around the area.

"Some bitch who works at the bar," he says, and Mikhail makes him hurt again for that crass language.

"Nikki," Mikhail says. "Her name is Nikki."

"S-sorry! He says if you turn over the girl and this

friend of yours out here dies, all is forgiven, and you get her—Nikki—back."

"Final question. Where are Gregor and Nikki now?" Mikhail asks. "Answer well, and your suffering will end."

"An expensive hotel… in the city. Says you'd never dare show there," and Mikhail just ends the man's life without a word more, sinking his knife into the man's heart before my eyes.

"What—why?" I ask, shocked.

"He was a goner and he knew it. It is less painful this way, at least. And I know where Gregor is," Mikhail says, wiping off his knife on the man's clothes before standing up.

Petyr returns just in time, and the two men exchange knowing nods.

There are still intricacies I don't understand. I might have killed someone in self-defense, but I'm not like these two. They were born into blood and violence and mayhem, and I was only recently adopted into it.

But I'm not afraid anymore. And if Nikki is a friend of Mikhail's, and she's been put at risk because of me, then there's no way I'm going to back down. No innocent is going to die on my behalf.

"What do we do?"

"Gregor has to die," Mikhail says, and Petyr nods to his words.

"The sooner the better. Otherwise we have a full blown civil war within the Bratva. And nobody will be getting out cleanly," Petyr says, and Mikhail nods in agreement. "I will take your girl with me, keep her safe while you do the job," he says, deciding things as clear as that. But there's no way I'm going to be pushed aside again!

"No," Mikhail says even before I can speak up. "Leave her to me," he says, and the two men exchange a look before shaking hands. "*Dos vedanya* old friend, I will see this through."

"And when it's done, I'll see to it you're where you belong," Petyr says before the two of them part, and it's just us again.

I look up at Mikhail, relief and apprehension mixing in my gut. This is real. We're making it real. Part of me knows that I have a choice, and that I could simply run away and let him handle it. Even if I left, I know Mikhail would never let Nikki or me get hurt.

But another part of me feels like I'm riding a water slide, unable to stop or slow down, and even though I'm frightened, there's no turning back.

"We're going back to where this all began, *kotika*," Mikhail says to me.

"How did you know he meant this hotel?" I ask, feeling a strange sensation as I sit outside the hotel where my whole life changed.

"Gregor knows I never set foot back at the scene of a hit. Especially not one as big as this with an ongoing investigation. He thinks he's safe from me here, because the increased security will make it impossible for me to get in without being detected and recognized," he explains, and that all makes too much sense.

It's past midnight, time crawling by as we race back to

the city, and I'm still wearing my messy mix of his clothes and mine.

"So how are we going to do this?" I ask.

WALKING INTO THE HOTEL, I feel an uncanny sense of *deja vu*. Even though I wasn't really fully conscious the entire time I was here before, I know it. And I have a queasy feeling in my stomach.

What happened here—and especially what *almost* happened here—turns my stomach.

I'm holding a coat over one arm and wearing a dress that fits not quite perfectly, but near about. My hair is done back in an emergency ponytail. Where Mikhail got the dress in such short notice, I didn't ask, but I put it on.

So here I am, dismissing the approaching concierge as I make my way to the elevator with my best attempt to appear like yet another lady arriving late. I know what they must think, I'm either some young kept girl coming back after a late night or a sex worker heading up to a client. But that's kind of the point: to be dismissively ignored as a part of the usual guests.

Each floor up is agony, and I feel my heart beating like loud drums, foretelling a coming doom.

Once I arrive at the floor Mikhail told me about, the very same one he plucked me from that bloody night, I see at the end of the hall two men in dark suits clearly standing guard. Another one is pacing the hall. And all three see me immediately.

I push down my fear, though, and I walk ahead.

Stick to the plan, my inner voice tells me. So I stick to the plan.

The three men all stare at me, not sure what to make of my approach at first. But then one of them mutters into a microphone pinned to his jacket and two doors open alongside me. More men pour out around me, and one immediately blocks off my way back.

Why did I propose this? Why did I insist?! This is madness! A voice in my head screams, but it's too late to back out.

I stop in front of the two guards at the big, double-door.

"I have a message for Gregorovich." My voice sounds surprisingly calm, in control. My mind is chaos, but I don't betray my inner fears. "It's important," I say when they hesitate.

But their eyes dart away, and it's just as Mikhail said. They're being watched too. For all the security this place brings them, the cameras prevent them from gunning me down or forcing me into anything then and there. It's a double-edged sword, as he said. Hems both them and me in.

One of the men takes hold of my arm, and though he tries to make it look harmless, his grip is tight. I immediately struggle, make a big show of it for the cameras as Mikhail instructed.

"He has to meet me out here," I say as the guard relents. "I want to talk in the hall about an exchange. Just him and I."

"*Nyet,*" says one of the men immediately. "The boss will not see anyone privately."

"Very well," I say, licking my lips as if thinking about it. But Mikhail told me they'd say this. Thankfully, they're predictable, and my boyfriend knows them better than anyone else. "One of you can remain. But has to stay at the end of the hall. For my safety."

"*Nyet*," he says again, but then he pauses, seeming to listen to something coming from his earpiece. "*Da. Da*," he says then instructs the other men with simple hand gestures, and they all begin to walk away, returning to side rooms until there's just the one head guard and me. "I must frisk you first," he says.

I walk a few paces away to the most open area of the hall, there I hold out my arms, put my feet apart a bit as the man moves in, patting his big, grubby hands over me. Every second is torture and reminds me of what Mikhail really saved me from, but I don't even quiver.

How am I handling this so well? Even as he cops a feel of my ass, just to show to me he can get away with it or put me on edge, I don't sway. He's going to get his, and soon.

The whole time, my heart is beating faster than it ever had before. No marathon can tax that muscle as hard as it is now. But I never show it. I kept my cool, my face stony and calm.

The thug who frisked me merely rises up and backs away without a word, opening the double-doors for his boss. Gregorovich.

The man who wanted me—wants me—tortured and killed. The man who made it so that I have nightmares of blood.

The man who gave me Mikhail.

It's a twisted emotion, to loathe someone and yet be grateful for how all their horribleness opened me up to so many amazing things.

Yet this is my first time ever seeing him, and he's not at all what I expect. He might even be handsome and charming, if he weren't grinning at me deviously, the mastermind of all my pain and fears.

And he didn't come with Nikki.

"Very brave of you to come all this way alone," he says to me in his Russian accent. "Or is your little boyfriend around here somewhere?" he asks, making an act of looking around, as if Mikhail were some imp hiding behind one of the fancy tables lining the hall.

"I'm not going to let an innocent woman take my place, no matter what Mikhail wants," I say firmly and with conviction. It surprises Gregorovich a little, but not much. He's leering again in no time in that ivory colored suit of his, one hand in his pocket. No doubt grasping a gun.

"How noble. But I don't think that dyke is as innocent as you believe," he says, and I take back everything I said about him. He's a creepy, greasy piece of shit, and no one could ever find him attractive after more than a few moments with him. "You don't hang around bad men for that long without being a little bad yourself, hm?"

I want to hit him, then and there.

"If you let her walk on out of here now, I'll come with you inside. That's a fair offer. And a no-brainer," I say firmly, sticking my chin up as I stand there in my blue dress. "I'm the one you want, after all."

He stares at me a while, and I can almost see the nasty thoughts playing out in his head being broadcast through his eyes like projectors at a theater. It's enough to make me feel like I need a long, scalding shower.

"I could just have you both right now, what would stop me?" he says.

"Why would you want to bother?" I counter. "This is much easier. Fewer chances of being caught," I say, gesturing to a camera in the corner.

That really gets him, because he grins so wide it almost looks genuine. Mikhail says that's how you know this creep is on the ropes. When he really pours on the deceit.

"Very well," he says, then speaks into his own communicator. "Bring her out."

We wait a moment, staring at one another. But when she doesn't immediately appear, he grows quickly anxious and turns to the door, cursing into his mic. "What's the hold up? Is that dyke struggling again?"

"That word is fucking gross..." I hiss under my breath, unable to contain my annoyance at him for a second. Which was dumb of me, I know—it drew attention back to me when I least needed it.

When I was pulling the sharp blade from my hair, used like a hair stick pin.

He turns to mock me just as the lights go out all around us, and I plunge the pointed tip at him.

I'm blind, he's blind, everything is impenetrable blackness but for the lights of the city outside through the windows at the end of the hall. But I know I hit him, I could feel the dagger plunge in.

"*Piz'da!*" he cries out, and he lashes out at me. I take a blow to the side of my head that knocks me aside, but it's nothing serious. I stumble in the dark and my eyes focus enough to make out his silhouette. And most noticeably, the dagger stuck through the palm of his one hand.

My disgust with his name-calling had given him time to raise his hand in defense. But I'm not sure that this was a better result for him than my original target anyhow.

The door to Gregor's room opens, and in the inky blackness, the man I just stabbed raises his gun and fires into the nothingness wildly. The second pointed dagger in my hair had fallen to the floor when I pulled out the first, but keeping my cool, I use Gregor's distraction to fumble on the carpet for it.

It's easier said than done, and just as I find it, he turns his attention back to me.

"*Piz'da!*" he says again, but from out of the darkness looms Mikhail's wraith-like shadow once more. And he puts a bullet through Gregor's unwounded hand, making him cry out as his gun clatters to the floor. He screams in pain.

It's my moment. That shot of Mikhail's wasn't a miss, he was giving me my opportunity. And I intend to use it.

Grasping the thin stiletto dagger in my hand, I jerk it up at him, stabbing it into his inner thigh. Then again I thrust it, this time piercing his groin. Then again. And again. Until the larger man falls over, and I climb atop him.

From that vantage point I can see the glint of fear in his eyes, as the city lights cast inwards, and I know we have the floor to ourselves. Mikhail never fails, and the way he confidently stands behind me indicates he did his job well and used all the time I bought him to eliminate Gregor's goons.

"Take your life back," Mikhail says to me in his deep husk. "It's your choice how." And he rests his hand upon my shoulder reassuringly.

We talked about it briefly when planning this.

I've shot men before, twice now. Even killed one myself. But that was self-defense. Strict and simple. A life to save a life in the moment. Stabbing a wounded man to death as my lover steps on his arm and pins him down, however…

That's a choice. A dark choice.

A choice about what type of woman I want to be, or could be.

I've maimed him, and I've made him suffer for what he's done to me and Mikhail and Eva and Nikki, for all the collateral damage that he's accumulated in what Mikhail told me was an unsanctioned power play.

None of this should have happened, and none of it would have happened, if not for Gregorovich, this disgusting creep beneath me.

But I'm not Mikhail. I know what needs to be done, but I can't be the one to do it.

He must sense me wavering, because his hand squeezes my shoulder in a reassuring manner. "It's okay."

He helps me up, and Gregor lays there, looking confused.

"Now wh-" he starts to say, but the sound of Mikhail's gun firing a muffled shot through its silencer ends him before he can finish his question.

Gregor can't live. Too many people would suffer and die if he did. But Mikhail will shoulder that burden for me.

"Let's go," he says, picking my coat up off the floor and draping it around my blood spattered dress as Nikki emerges from the room, looking skittish and scared.

"It's all over now," I assure her.

CHAPTER 23

—————

ALICIA

THREE YEARS LATER

I t's the anniversary of the night that Mikhail and I met, three years ago now. We never really celebrate it, it'd feel crass to do so, but we always take note of it and do something a little special. I'm not sure what Mikhail has in mind for me this year, though. He's been so busy after taking over for Gregorovich as *Avtoritet*. But then, I've been busy too.

Leon bops in my lap, our oldest son, named after Mikhail's brother. Already two and growing like a weed. Having two kids makes it a bit hard to concentrate on managing all of Mikhail's financial records, but I like being involved in his business. And out of danger. Besides, he says I'm the one person he can trust.

I glance out over at Central Park, spread out before me from our beautiful condo. It's a place bigger than I ever could have dreamed I'd live in, but with the two kids, plus mom and Hernando, it's just perfect. Plenty of privacy and space, and the best location, right in the center of every-thing. It's a commute for Mikhail, of course, but he wanted to keep his growing family somewhere safe. And in New York, safe means ritzy.

"Mommy, walk," Leon says, squirming down from my lap and rushing to Eva's playpen. He's a bright kid, and I blame that on his dad. Mikhail has been reading to him every night since before he was even born, I guess trying to be the father he never had. Regardless of his reasons, I couldn't be more proud of our little family.

"How about nan takes you for your walk," I say as I pick Eva up, bringing her down the hall. My mom has recovered a lot since meeting Hernando, and the doctors have said it's a miracle, but I know what it actually is. He's given her purpose again, never treated her like an old lady knocking on death's door. After dad died, I guess she lost a lot of that spark, but Hernando has lit her back up.

"Oh my little Eva!" Mom says as she comes to collect my baby from my arms.

"Could you take her and Leon for a little walk in Central Park? Mikhail is due home soon, and I have a little surprise for him."

My mom laughs, bouncing Eva in her arms as she nods.

"Of course, sweet peach. We'll get out of your hair for a bit!" She kisses me on the cheek before she quickly gathers the children and leaves me to the silence.

It's funny, living so high above the bustle of New York, away from the crowds and the noise. Mikhail splurged on this place, most of his savings gone into securing the best condo he could find, our little castle from which to rule. But as a boss in the Bratva, the millions he spent on this place seem like peanuts. I should know, I do the books.

I head into our bedroom, changing out of my more

comfortable clothes into a slinky red dress that looks similar to the one that Mikhail first found me in, and I tie my hair back, letting a couple tendrils frame my face. I'm used to dressing up fancy now, and it doesn't take a lot of time to put on my makeup and the finishing touches.

By the time I finish, though, I hear the door unlocking. Even after all this time, I find my hand going to the gun hidden in my vanity, instincts kicking in before I hear Mikhail's voice. He knows better than to surprise me after trying that once on our wedding night and finding me with a gun in my hands pointed at his chest.

"You're home," I smile as I head into the living room to greet him.

His face lights up with warmth as we greet, and the beautiful bouquet of flowers he whips out from behind his back helps. The assortment was carefully picked, including several white gardenias, the flowers I'd begged for at our wedding. I didn't care about anything else, but gardenias were my dad and mom's wedding flower, and he got her one every anniversary. Now the tradition has been passed down.

"I stopped off for these, *kotika*," he says, and simple acts like that I know are far more troublesome now. He has a small army of guards with him wherever he goes. Though none of that keeps him from being sweet to me, like how he's sweeping me up in his arm and pulling me in for a deep, passionate kiss.

The fire between us hasn't dimmed at all as we make out, and before our greeting can be completed, my beautiful new flowers are fallen to the floor despite my best efforts, my red dress is crumpled beside it, and I am glistening with perspiration with my stunning, muscular hunk on top of me.

"It tortures me the whole day through to have to wait to ravage you," he growls, plucking another kiss from my lips in our post-coital bliss.

I curl into him, knowing my hair and makeup is a mess, but I don't care. Nothing could be more perfect than this moment as my mouth meets his, slower and lazier. I want to remember this moment, the light scent of flowers filling my senses, the feel of his heavy hands on my waist.

Then I lightly rub the back of his hand, guiding it lower, towards my navel, and I catch his eyes.

"I have good news," I say, unable to resist smiling. My love was so virile and potent, we never needed to wait long for a new life to begin within me.

His face lights up just like it did the first time I told him I was expecting.

"Boy or girl, I hope this one is as amazing as you, my love. My life," he says, overjoyed with the prospect of being a father the third time over.

THANK YOU FOR READING! You may sign up for my newsletter to be notified when I have a new release on the way: http://alexisabbott.com/newsletter

~Alexis Abbott

GLOSSARY

Avtoritet - The Authority, the Boss

Kotika - Kitty cat

Nichego - Nothing

Klyanus - I swear

Zasranec - Asshole

Da, da, moy drug - Yes yes, my friend

Podruga - Girlfriend

Politsiya - Police

Khorosho - Alright

Devushka - Girl

Sotrudnik - Officer

Mudak - Asshole/dickhead

Chert voz'mi - Damn it

Byet ostorozhen - Carefully

Zatk'nis, mu'dak - Dumb asshole

Pidarasy - vacation

Vy prekrasny - Beautiful

Obeshchayu - I promise

Ne volnuytes, kroshka - It's okay, baby

Ochyen priyatno, sestra - Nice to meet you, sister
Moy brat - My brother
Bratishka - Little brother
Pozhaluysta - Please
Smelaya devushka - Daring girl
Sestra - Sister
Spasibo - Thank you
Da svidaniya - Goodbye
Fsyevo harosheva - Safe travels
Pizdoon - Fucking liar
Bozhe moi - My God!
Piz'da - Cunt
Govnjúk - Bastard / Shithead
Spetsnaz - Russian Special Forces
Nyet - No
Da - Yes

Connect with Alexis

Get an EXCLUSIVE book, **FREE** just as a thank you for signing up for my newsletter! Plus you'll never miss a new release, cover reveal, or promotion!

http://alexisabbott.com/newsletter

facebook.com/abbottauthor

twitter.com/abbottauthor

instagram.com/alexisabbottauthor

amazon.com/Alexis-Abbott/e/B013YL5290

bookbub.com/authors/alexis-abbott

pinterest.com/badboyromance

About the Author

Alexis Abbott is a Wall Street Journal & USA Today best-selling author who writes about dangerous men and the women who love them. If you can't resist a bad boy who is a good man, you just found your next addiction. With heart-stopping action, mouth watering sex, and passionate romances that will leave you breathless, Alexis Abbott writes romantic thrillers like no one else can.

When she's not writing your next book boyfriend, you'll find her living a real life romance novel with her own bad boy soulmate in Bonavista, NL, Canada.

Thank you for reading! You may sign up for my newsletter to be notified when I have a new release on the way:

http://alexisabbott.com/newsletter

~Alexis Abbott

---

facebook.com/abbottauthor

twitter.com/abbottauthor

instagram.com/alexisabbottauthor

amazon.com/Alexis-Abbott/e/B013YL5290

bookbub.com/authors/alexis-abbott

pinterest.com/badboyromance

ALSO BY ALEXIS ABBOTT

<u>Romantic Suspense:</u>

HITMEN SERIES:

Owned by the Hitman

Sold to the Hitman

Saved by the Hitman

Captive of the Hitman

Stolen from the Hitman

Hostage of the Hitman

Taken by the Hitman

The Hitman's Masquerade (Short Story)

HEARTBREAKERS MC

Breaker

Bones

Ironside

Big Daddy

THE KILLER TRILOGY:

Book 1: Killer for Hire

Book 2: Killer Desire

Book 3: Killer on Fire

HOSTAGES:

Trafficked

Stealing Her

The Assassin's Heart

Killing For Her

Abducted

Stolen Jewel

Possessive

Killers:

Hunter's Baby

I Hired A Hitman

Stepbrothers:

Ruthless

Criminal

Glitz & Grit:

Betting on Love

Vegas Boss

Rock Hard Bodyguard

Innocence For Sale: Jane

Redeeming Viktor

Sexy SEALs

Sweetheart for the SEAL

Sights on the SEAL

<u>BDSM Romance:</u>

Bound as the World Burns (SFF)

ACKNOWLEDGMENTS

Thank you to my amazing Patrons. I'm constantly humbled and grateful for your support.

Ramona Cabrera
Melissa Hedrick
Virginia Swanson
Dawn Daughenbaugh
Don Doss
Stacie Currie

If you'd like to join them — and get my ebooks or paperbacks — you can find me here on Patreon.
https://www.patreon.com/alexisabbott

www.ingramcontent.com/pod-product-compliance
Lightning Source LLC
Chambersburg PA
CBHW021141190726
48288CB00008B/2760